The Revenant Runner

Steven Popoford and the

Burrowed Serpent

A Popoford's Run Thriller

Book Three

"Much will be required of the person entrusted with much,

and still more will be demanded of the person entrusted with more." LK 12:48

by Robert Wood Anderson

Tautly Sharp Publishing

Robert Wood Anderson
c/o Tautly Sharp Publishing
PO Box 1566
Bellevue, NE 68005-1566
https://rwanderson-author.com/klfp
rwa@rwanderson-author.com

Publisher's Note: This is a work of fiction. Except for historical names, heavenly spirits, and demons, all names, characters, places, and incidents are a product of the author's imagination. Locales and public names are sometimes used for atmospheric purposes. Any resemblance to actual people, living or dead, or to businesses, companies, events, institutions, or locales is entirely coincidental.

Book Layout © 2017 BookDesignTemplates.com

The Revenant Runner/ Robert Wood Anderson -- 1st ed.
ISBN 978-1-7347698-8-3

For a copy of the first two

Popoford Run books,

please visit Amazon with this link:

Acknowledgments

J/M/J

To My Dear Wife

"She was the miracle God had sent to save him. She was the model the Blessed Virgin Mary placed before his eyes. He adored and honored her not as a saint but as an imitation of life bravely and righteously lived. Their love was ordained."

For contributions to my worldview and references to their work:

C. S. Lewis, Joe Mobley, Joe Allen, Patrick K. O'Donnell, Jasper Fforde, Aleksandr Solzhenitsyn, St. Paul, Dante Alighieri, Cardinal Timothy M. Dolan, Bishop Robert Barron, Charles Dickens, Bill Gertz, Mark Levin, The Catechism of the Catholic Church, The Blessed Virgin Mary, The Holy Trinity, Steven K. Bannon, Dr. Wilhelms, Hoyt Axton, Taj Mahal, Ben Harnwell, Saint Pope John Paul II

> "In peace there's nothing so becomes a man,
> As modest stillness and humility;
> But when the blast of war blows in our ears,
> Then imitate the action of the tiger:
> Stiffen the sinews, conjure up the blood,
> Disguise fair nature with hard-favoured rage:
> Then lend the eye a terrible aspect;
> Let it pry through the portage of the head,
> Like the brass cannon; let the brow o'erwhelm it
> As fearfully as doth a galled rock
> O'erhang and jutty his confounded base,

– ROBERT WOOD ANDERSON

Swill'd with the wild and wasteful ocean.
Now set the teeth and stretch the nostril wide;
Hold hard the breath and bend up every spirit
To his full height."
Henry V, Act III, Scene I, William Shakespeare

CHAPTER ONE

It was a black hole concealed in the depths of an abysmally dank architectural horror, a splendid example of the modern, perniciously minimalist mistake. Grey slabs pierced with trapezoid holes mimicking gunner's ports served as windows yet let in precious little light. The floors from the basement to the top floor were strewn with scrap paper labeled "Top Secret."

No one protected the halls of Section 33. No one cared. The agency had been brought to its knees three years earlier, and its concealed secrets were no longer valuable. But the shriveled biped that sat in his unique chair five feet off the floor was oblivious to his accommodations. His synapses were focused on the chart he had drawn on his green chalkboard.

His white-on-green masterpiece was everything to him, so much so that he didn't hear the elevator door opening in the third sub-basement where he lived and worked. Nor did he see the shadow cast on the wall behind his chalkboard, nor did he hear the steps slowly advancing, toe, heel, toe, heel, toe, heel.

When he sensed the intruder and froze in his chair, he was startled by the hand reaching around and pressing his head against his cushioned seatback. There was no time for terror. The straight razor swiped a clean slice from ear to ear, severing his carotid arteries and slicing his vocal cords.

The dwarf was peaceful in dying, for the last thing he saw was the mistake in his formula. The error he had been searching for these three years. He was thrilled that he had solved the problem and confident no one else could understand what he had just discovered.

He tried but failed to sing a remembered childhood tune as he bled out. It was the one that the nuns had taught him when he had first been given up to them:

> Jesus Loves Me, this I know.
> For the Bible tells me so.
> Little lambs to Him belong.
> We are weak, and He is strong.
> Yes, Jesus Loves Me.
> Yes, Jesus Loves Me.
> Yes, Jesus Loves Me.
> The Bible Tells me so.

The scent of frankincense and myrrh filled his nostrils and its pungent smoke wrapped around his distorted face, stinging his eyes as life passed to death, judgment, and eternity.

His assassin snapped a picture of the chalkboard and made a call.

A phone rang in a darkened office three thousand miles away. An iridescent wrinkled hand shimmering with a weakening inner light reached for the receiver and tentatively raised it to withered lips. The wretched creature did not speak, but his gurgling breath and slow exhalation were enough for the caller to begin his report.

"The dwarf is dead—photo proof on the way along with the formula. The location has been cleaned. There will be no evidence remaining. I'll send you details, and you will find identification in his apartment when you arrive. I was paid in full. You know where you can reach me whenever you have further need of my services."

The killer ended the call, and the Black Angel's malignant servant replaced the receiver and turned his chair to the window. There he saw the lights a-sparkle, the shimmering dots so cherished by men yet insignificant compared to the Godhead's beams most intimately feared by him. Still, none of his terrors mattered, for he was a soul wholly-owned, a slave returned from the underworld to complete what he had left undone.

He tried to close his eyelids in the stupor of rebirth, but the city lights kept coming. His lids had not yet developed muscular connections and could not be controlled.

From within the blackness of his overhanging hood, he felt his lips maturing from withered husks to supple tools exquisitely eager to speak artful lies of craft, cunning, and deceit. His mind was racing ahead out of his desire to please his master.

He forced himself to relax and dissolved his desirous longing into a dew of patient faith. For he was the one sent, the one named to deliver the lingering faithful to the master of the fire pit and eternal hopelessness. He was the chosen one sent to ensnare the world in his master's name. He had been known as Simon Contlerust in a previous incarnation, having taken on the body of the dead former Home Office operative. His new human form was slowly emerging, one trait at a time.

He made a quarter-turn away from the window and caught slices of his image reflected in a large mirror. The city daubed an evolving light picture in reflection, and he marveled at the transformation of the black spirit he saw before him. It was not the image of mortal beauty. Instead, it was a cluster of amorphous cells devoid of grace and compounding by the second into a creature that only a dead mother could love. It was a hideous sight yet gloriously pitiful. In reflection, the tiny creature he saw began as a strapping young man but was soon reduced into a compressed, short-legged, barrel-chested dwarf.

His head, elegant at first glance, evolved into a solid Balkan cube: ears protruding and large eyes emphasized by perpetually startled eyebrows. These static attributes countered his silvery-thin skin that appeared to be sliding off his face, hampered only by a solid attachment to the deflated bags under his eyes. His lips were puffy and pale, his throat a stack of pancakes. He was transformed.

His phone signaled an incoming message, and he reached for it, missing it by a foot though his arm was fully outstretched. Bending closer to the desk, he managed to activate the screen.

The first image was a full-face, sliced-throat shot suitable for the morgue. The second was its companion shot showing the dwarf genius's whole body.

The evil spirit returned his gaze to the mirror and contemplated his situation. It was perfect irony. His master had sent him, and here he would do his master's bidding. Not with splendid beauty, but with infirmity. Not as a pampered fool but as a brilliant castaway.

Yet even as he began to play the unfortunate, his brain reached a cognitive threshold where he could distinguish between accepted norms and actualities.

The murdered dwarf was an honored genius, no matter his appearance. No matter how closely he had been held secretly to the chest of America's espionage universe, his public existence was denied, dismissed, and scorned. He knew it was neither the nature of the man nor the rouge on his powdered face that marked him a man and not a fool. It was the grit of his heart, wit, and wisdom of his mind that made the difference. The dwarf had been a man.

His master knew where he would have the most significant leverage: Contlerust would find the solution to the scientist's formula. Then, from the depth of his corrupt mind, Contlerust would wreak havoc upon the world—all for his prince.

His master demanded absolute loyalty without expectation of reward, and his servant was ineligible for false promises. Such pledges were reserved for the yet-to-be damned.

His master had equipped him with the power to guide, seduce, and corrupt all that he laid his eyes upon. Earth was his playground, and nothing but failure conjured fear in his black soul.

CHAPTER TWO

Eight months earlier, Sarah Tufftang was having a difficult pregnancy. She had just entered her second trimester, and her latest sonogram had exposed possible anomalies. She was carrying a boy whose head was slightly larger than the norm. Though Down Syndrome had been ruled out, encephalitis was suspected. A nurse practitioner had given Sarah some advice.

"If you're afraid the child will have brain damage or be deformed, now is the time to consider abortion."

Sarah's response cleared the room, and her doctor rushed in and guided her into his office.

"How dare you suggest killing my baby!" Sarah shouted. "Are you a physician or a state executioner?"

"Miss Tufftang, I take the meaning of my oath from the original text and repudiate the revisionary versions. I do not suggest nor condone abortion for the convenience of anyone. If you were in mortal danger, I would do all I could to save you and your baby. The nurse was out of line to mention abortion."

"You better keep her away from me!"

"I intend to dismiss her."

Sarah hadn't responded but sat silently as the doctor continued.

"I expect you to have a normal delivery, Miss Tufftang. His cranial volume is indeed decidedly large. He'll probably be brilliant. I see nothing to worry about. If you follow my advice, you should have a beautiful baby in your arms in three months."

Sarah had let a smile grow, and her body relaxed.

"You'll have your hands full with this one," he said. "Teach him to be a good boy and be patient with others. He may well be a genius."

The boy's father was Simon Contlerust, who had died in circumstances still unclear to her. Contlerust's daughter, Millie, had been a lifeline in those early months. Recently, however, their phone calls had begun to dwindle as Millie became consumed in marriage preparations. Sarah was alone and lonely with only one friend at Claramon College in Merced, California. Dean Wrenbutt, her boss, was that friend.

Once well known as "Dean Letch," an opportunist among the free-wheeling student neophytes, Wrenbutt had made a remarkable about-face. A Resurrection Runner mind-wipe administered by Steven Popoford made him a devout adherent to the Constitution and the rule of law and strengthened his moral code. Sarah gave him a call as she left the doctor's office.

Thornton Wrenbutt was quietly in love with Sarah Tufftang, but he had no reason to believe she had similar feelings about him. His was an avuncular relationship he accepted out of fear of estrangement.

"How did your doctor visit go?" he asked.

"Ugly and beautiful," she said. "Some people are swine. Others are better."

"Is the baby okay?"

"That's what I want to talk about. But don't worry. He's good."

"Oh. You had me going for a minute."

"Sorry," Sarah said. "I have a lot on my mind."

"All right," Wrenbutt said. "Can you come to my office? I have a meeting in an hour and would like to stay here."

"Sure. I'll be there in ten minutes."

Sarah hung up as she got into her car. She took a deep breath and slowly exhaled. Thank God Thornton was there. She didn't know who she could turn to without him except Millie and Steven. But she didn't want to bother them. As she pulled into a visitor parking slot, a smile brightened her expression, and she saw Dean Wrenbutt standing on the curb, smiling back. He had turned out to be a good guy.

They walked to the History building, climbed the stairs, and entered the dean's front office, where Wrenbutt's secretary was sitting at her desk. She was a pleasant young woman who had replaced Miss Shlenterby, a sourpuss.

Sitting dreamy-eyed on the visitor's couch was a man in his forties. Natty and slight, his eyes never left the secretary. He resembled a trained dog waiting patiently and expectantly at the proper time for his noon-time meal. Wrenbutt had become used to him hanging out in his office and expected to find puddles of drool on the floor every day after the man had finally left.

His name was Professor Erik Mendaycik, accent on the "day." He was a professor of Experimental Cognitive Neuroscience working on top-secret government research. He appeared to have nothing better to do with his lunchtime than fawn over the girl.

"Any messages for me, Miss Underdown?"

"Why no, Sir," she said in a phony drawl. "Y'all've had a quiet day so far."

Wrenbutt glanced at Mendaycik without speaking as he entered his inner office. Sarah was a bit more polite.

"Any breakthroughs, Erik?" She called him by his first name, mainly because he insisted on being called doctor, a title she held herself but reserved for physicians.

Mendaycik never took his eyes off Miss Underdown and only nodded dismissively.

Sarah closed Wrenbutt's office door and allowed a little laugh to escape. The dean let loose a bellow that could have been heard all over campus if his doors hadn't been closed.

"Isn't he special?" Wrenbutt's sarcasm was pronounced. "Very high and mighty."

"Self-proclaimed," Sarah added.

Wrenbutt smiled. "So it is with men seeking God's powers. This one would eliminate the human race as we know it with his eye still fixed on the creation of man-made evolution. He proposes melding human frailty with algorithmic imperfection to classify easily, relegate, monitor, and employ all souls in their needed roles. This new soul, he says, is not a fancy of God-fearing men but is the required truth of global peace."

"Oh, he's high-minded," Sarah said. "You can see it in his lecherous eyes."

Sarah sat on the couch across from Wrenbutt's desk, and her expression rapidly altered. Instead of the assured and steady-eyed composure of a tenured professor of political history, her skin stretched tight as she clenched her teeth and drew her mouth into a wrinkled frown. Her eyes began to tear, and soon she dropped her head into her hands and sobbed uncontrollably.

Thornton was flummoxed. In earlier days, he would have taken advantage of the situation: an emotionally decomposing woman vulnerable and within reach was his favorite dream in days past. But not now. Those prurient days of soulless opportunity were gone, washed away by mind-bending drugs that left only a fantasy behind in his altered memory. In short, he was a changed man: a bit pompous, a bit more unattractive, and a lot more reliable.

Instead of sitting on the couch with her, Wrenbutt pulled a chair up and sat facing her.

"Do you want to talk about it," was all he said, and Sarah looked up at him.

"I'm so afraid."

"What did the doctor say about your boy."

It was the first time Sarah had heard anyone call her unborn baby 'her boy.' She broke down in tears. "Oh, Jesus," she sputtered. "You take care of it."

Wrenbutt was unable to find the words he thought he needed to say. In time, he made a quiet pronouncement that simply confirmed Sarah's wish and showed himself to be her friend in need. "He will."

Sarah raised her head while blotting her eyes with the back of her hands. The look on Wrenbutt's face was enough to cause a deep sigh to escape her mouth. She smiled hesitantly and reached out for his hand. "My friend, she said," and he gave her hand a warm squeeze.

CHAPTER THREE

Steven Popoford stepped out of the shower. He toweled himself dry and looked into the fogged mirror with a critical eye. He was pleased with what he saw until he wiped the fog vapor from the glass. With a clear view of himself, he scowled at his body's condition. Though not vainglorious, it was a narcissistic inventory, for he recognized what others might miss. He was tipping forward into an aging freefall. A destabilization of his body had begun. His belly and chest were starting a symbolic changing of the guard. His pects were not as sinewy as they once were, and his belly was getting a roundness that would become a paunch in due course if he let it go.

He had just turned thirty-three and had a more critical eye for his conditioning than anyone else. But he was a pragmatist, and knowing that a little less eating and a slightly longer calisthenic regimen would reverse his slackened condition, he instantly committed to upping his exercise game. He had another reason. He wasn't alone in his house in Whimsy, a place a little large for one person and perhaps too small for two. Now, he shared it with sublime pleasure with his wife, Millie.

He stepped into the bedroom and smiled at the woman he'd shared his bed with for the first time the night before. Their romance had begun in this little house.

Millie C. Popoford did not return his smile, for she continued to sleep as he had left her, softly breathing, a sheet covering her body yet revealing every contour he had enjoyed throughout their honeymoon night.

He was as quiet as he could be as he put on his underwear and reflected on a day months before when they'd returned to his house after Millie had killed the man who had impersonated her father. It seemed they were free of all the horror, betrayal, and repugnance they had endured since then.

They'd talked into the early morning about what had happened and what they were to do. Popoford had proposed, and Millie had accepted without hesitation.

"When I marry you, Steven Popoford, I will come to you untouched. It is something I decided on long ago. We must wait and be married in the church."

Popoford had composed himself and reluctantly agreed.

Father Logan guided them in their six-month matrimonial discernment and, at the same time, Popoford's renewal in the faith. They were finally married at the Chapel of the Blessed Virgin in Elgin Base.

It was a small ceremony. Neither of them had any friends except for Sarah Tufftang, who was six months pregnant and unable to travel due to complications. Sheriff George Florter, Gert Marshall, and Joe at Joe's Bar were dead, so Popoford had no one to stand up for him. Millie's family was non-existent.

There was a flower girl who was the granddaughter of the church secretary and a feeble custodian present as witnesses. The Chapel's boys choir, consisting of two pubescent sopranos, and a fifteen-year-old bass, provided the music. The best that could be said for them was that they were sincere, and one of them could keep the pitch, and it wasn't the bass.

But theirs was not a lonely wedding, for all they saw was themselves, chaste in the eyes of God and committed to a prayerful life together. Their hearts were full of joy and at peace. They started their lives together without clutter, misery, or guilt. Innocent as roses, their kiss cemented their eternal union. Come what may, they were bound to one another as one body and one soul.

"We will always be together," he told her.

"Yes, always," she said.

CHAPTER FOUR

Popoford walked to the kitchen as quietly as he could. He made a pot of coffee and waited for it to perk. Then he smiled at a picture of The Blessed Virgin Mary he had hanging on the wall and turned towards the one window at the front of the house. He searched the woods on the other side of their gravel-covered clearing. He counted ten hens and two longbeards in the turkey rafter moving from behind the house toward the woods. As they approached the forest, their cluster collapsed into a single file line. Each of them flared their wings as they stepped off the gravel and followed the leader into the undergrowth.

Popoford smiled at the bucolic scene. Peace was his, a peace he had only dreamed of, a quiet never known, the gift of a lifetime. He was content but could not find the words to express his feeling. He just let the experience flow over him until the chuffing of the last percolator steam came to a hoarse end. The coffee was ready, and his first full day of married life had begun.

He wanted to let Millie sleep as long as she wanted. There was no need to wake her. They had no appointments or commitments.

He sat at the kitchen table where he had first met Millie and reminisced about that day.

She was alluring at first sight. He was shy. Even at his age, he was inexperienced. His earlier life had been a whipped custard of lies and destroyed memories. He was living in a cocoon of lost time, unprepared for her smoldering advances, her shameless desire. He fell for her right then and there at this table.

He bolted to his feet at a sudden knock on his front door. His cup tipped, and his coffee slopped on his clothes.

Brushing the hot liquid off his pants, he went to the door, grabbing a Sig P18 from the holster riveted to the wall. Paranoia ran deep in the retired assassin's blood. He raised the pistol to his only eye and slowly opened the door.

"Who is it?" he said as he peered out, expecting to see someone on the porch. "Who is it?" he repeated, but there was no answer.

Popoford took a two-handed grip on his gun and kicked the door wide open. What he saw confused him, and he let a split second pass without reacting, a split second that the dwarf standing in front of him used effectively to fire a dart into Popoford's chest.

The dwarf snatched Popoford's left wrist and sliced a short, longitudinal gash down his radial artery. Popoford's knees buckled, and he fell to his knees while his blood pumped rhythmically onto the floor.

He stared in disbelief, eye to eye with the dwarf. His lungs were sucking air when the man spoke.

"I once told you I'd be back for your arsenal, Steven. Too bad you thought I was dead. See you in Hell."

The last thing the newlywed ex-assassin saw while his good eye closed was the apparition of Simon Contlerust momentarily wrapped around the dwarf's face. Then it faded, and the dwarf's silvery-thin skin and block-shaped head filled Popoford's vision.

As he collapsed, the last thing he heard was Millie calling from the bedroom.

"Hey, lover! Come back!"

CHAPTER FIVE

Millie, lulled in sleep, finally threw off the sheets and sat on the edge of their bed. Her thoughts were on her husband. His body and hers were joined as if created for the other in tentative, innocent discovery. She wasn't surprised, for it was her conviction that husband and wife were one soul bound by their marriage sacrament ordained before the Creation. They were meant for each other.

She was pleased, and contentment warmed her soul. This was the best day of her life.

Millie finally stood up and grabbed the robe she had let fall from her shoulders the night before. She went to the bathroom and freshened up. Satisfaction and joy flowed through her as she stepped into their front room.

She was startled by a stray dog that had come in through the open front door. The cur was lapping up some dark liquid.

"Out!" she yelled. "Get out!"

The dog casually looked at her and bared its teeth. Its soft growl warned her to keep her distance. When it was sure it had won the standoff, the dog turned and trotted across the clearing and into the woods. It stopped and looked back at Millie and barked once. Then it strode into the shadows and disappeared. Popoford was nowhere to be seen.

"Steven!" Millie called, stepping out on the porch. "Steven! Come back inside. I have a surprise for you. Hurry up! I need you. Now!"

She heard the sounds of the trees swaying, and the birds singing and felt the light breeze that nuzzled her hair.

She smiled to herself and wondered what Popoford was up to. She called out for him again, but still, he didn't answer. She went inside and closed the door.

What she saw turned her warm soul to ice.

A cup was sitting in a small puddle of coffee on the kitchen table. There was coffee spilled on the floor as well.

Millie figured that Popoford had been startled by something or someone. It might have been the dog. It might have been anything.

She walked back towards the door and inspected the floor more thoroughly. There was a drop still there, a drop the dog had left behind when surprised.

Millie put her finger in the dark liquid and smelled its sweetness. She nearly fainted, but instead, she yanked the door open and ran into the clearing frantically screaming, hysterically calling out to her husband.

Millie knew the blood was his. The dog had been licking his blood!

Millie fell to her knees in the gravel clearing, sobbing and crying out to The Blessed Virgin to look after her husband.

In her devastation, she failed to see what was right in front of her.

A trail of disturbed gravel led from her door to the woods. In the shadows just beyond the tree line, the dog stood panting, staring her down, gradually transforming itself back into the dwarf. Beside the man-like creature lay the bloody body of Steven Popoford, her husband, the original Resurrection Runner.

CHAPTER SIX

Millie slumped on the gravel until her tears stopped and her spasmodic sobbing subsided. She was drained. Wrecked. A virtuous soul seeking an answer for her suffering. She sat up and collected her thoughts, composing her shattered heart.

Then, with a spirited will, she stood up and collected herself. She had never been a quitter. Giving up was for the lost. She wasn't lost, just crippled. Not destroyed, just ground to a pulp. Not done; just beginning to fight.

Her heart broke, but her faith stayed strong. She saw her mission written on stone tablets. Retribution was her cause: holy vengeance in Jesus' name.

"Thy will be done," she whispered as if sending her message on the wind for God and His enemies to hear.

She walked with a resolute purpose, slowly, like a matador might mesmerize his bull. It was the dance of death. She would survive though her hopes and dreams had been quenched as she slept, her future shortened to this moment.

Millie entered their house and stood silently for a moment, scanning the front room and the kitchen. Sadness nearly overwhelmed her as a vision of times not to be filled her head.

Popoford gave their little boy another spoonful of apple sauce at the kitchen table. The boy's bib was wet with drool, and his pink lips were oozing the breakfast overflowing from his mouth. Their darling child had his father's sincere eyes, his intense concentration. His mouth pouted in a way she recognized as Steven's. His ears were hers, pressing close to his head, and his hair was red. Then self-consciousness took hold of her dream, and the boy's father, Steven Popoford, faded into an apparition of lost hope. The child sat alone, eyes searching, crinkled in anxiety, and tears fell in two parallel streams down his rosy cheeks.

Millie scrunched her eyes closed and shook her head until the fantasy passed.

She recovered her wits and spun around where she stood, retrieving an electronic earbud from a box on top of a living room cabinet. She switched it on and immediately connected to Popoford's EID grid. The device rapidly completed a perimeter check, and a three-beep signal indicated that the property was secure.

Millie grabbed the shotgun above the front door and marched across the scrabbled gravel clearing to where she last saw the bloodthirsty dog enter the woods.

She was pissed at herself. For a second, she had given up! She had accepted her husband's death without proof. Now the hatred and revenge she had stoked in herself gave way to a righteous desire for knowledge of what had happened to the man she loved.

When Millie stepped onto the spongy loam, she looked both ways, hoping to find Popoford's tracks. There were distinguishable raccoon and deer tracks in the moist earth but no sign of Popoford's footsteps. Yet Millie's eyes were drawn to parallel troughs stretching into the woods. They were shallow and had rounded walls, and she thought the bare heels of someone being dragged into the trees could have made them.

A quiet beep informed her that the security system had picked up a signal.

"Single-subject acquired near the southeast boundary. Erratic, slow movement."

Millie froze and waited for the next report. The thirty-second pause took forever, and when the information finally came, it was a repetition: *"Single-subject acquired near the southeast boundary. Erratic, slow movement."*

Millie's heart leaped. That must be Steven!

She took off rapidly, keeping her eyes glued to the track. She'd traveled only twenty yards into the dark forest when the security system gave another report.

"Subject immobile. No vital signs reported."

Millie paused to take it in, but the information only made her more determined and anxious to find whoever or whatever it was at the end of the trail.

She slogged through the dank undergrowth, following the two muddy grooves and the trampled foliage accompanying them.

She was nearing the property's eastern boundary and sunlight shined through the thinning forest canopy and its perimeter. The road was just beyond.

Millie froze for a second and gasped.

A barefoot body was sprawled on the forest floor, a disheveled bathrobe exposing its backside to its shoulder blades.

It was her husband, Steven, lying face down in the mud.

CHAPTER SEVEN

His skivvies were dry: a good sign, but his red-on-white tank top was wet. His face was smushed into the pine needle overburden. His head had been stomped into the forest floor. The back of his legs, just above his knees, had dark hematoma blotches. His shoulders had been severely damaged: his left scapula was breaking through his skin, and his right clavicle was shattered, judging by the unnaturally twisted way his arm wrapped around his back. There were two holes in his tank top near his side. They were spaced apart about the width of the dog's canines. His lungs appeared to have been spared, but his ribs were undoubtedly shattered. He didn't move.

Millie fell to her knees. Terror clutched her heart, which was beating like a death knell, slow, rhythmic, and relentless. A scream welled up in her gut, and she was about to shatter the wilderness hush when she laid a hand on his throat as a final goodbye and felt a weak pulse in his carotid artery.

She gasped and fell to her knees, leaning over and pressing her ear to his back. She could barely hear his weak heartbeat and shallow breathing, but it was enough for an explosion of hope to invigorate her.

"You're alive, Steven!" she called out. "I've got to get you back to the house. Can you help me? Can you stand up?"

Popoford groaned softly, and Millie, struggling, finally rolled him on his back.

His body was even more damaged than she expected. The fang wounds were minor, but hematomas and contusions radiated from them, blotching his skin in symmetric swirls. It was as if poison had been injected, leaving necrotic tissue in its wake. The damage was worse than what Millie expected. But what worried her most was a pale-green discoloration slowly wending its way up his neck and terminating behind his right ear. Something was attacking his brain.

"Settle in for a bit, Steven," she said, suppressing her panic. "You're going to be alright. I just need to get the ATV and get you back to the house. Okay? Can you hang on for a few minutes?"

A meager smile formed on his lips.

"Hang on so I can be your wife for at least another day."

Millie jumped to her feet, and as she turned away, she heard a warning in her ear.

"Vehicle turning on drive, advancing to the clearing."

She ran as fast as she could through the woods scattering unseen wildlife and springing into the clearing just in time to watch the county sheriff drive up to the house. She retreated into the forest cover to watch.

The sheriff parked his patrol car, stepped out, scanned the area, and went to the front door Millie had left open.

"Anyone home?" he called.

Hearing no response, he walked around back and called again.

"Hey. It's me! Sheriff Dill. Anyone home?

Sheriff Langley Dill was a picklepuss, his face and lips all scrunched up and shaggy eyebrows wrinkling above rheumy eyes, bloodshot and popping out of sagging lower lids. His purple lips stretched into a cocked-up smile broad and thin on the left and a fatty sneer on the right. He had replaced Popoford's only friend, Sheriff Florter, murdered a year ago. Neither Popoford nor Millie knew much about him.

Hearing no response to his call, Dill returned to the clearing and reached into his car for his radio's microphone.

"Dill to base. Come in."

He waited, and soon, he received a reply.

"Base to Dill. Come in, Sheriff."

"Hey, Maddie. I'm up at Steven Popoford's place, and there's no one responding to my call. The front door's open. I'm just letting you know that I'm going inside. I have a suspicion that there's been foul play."

"We don't have a warrant, Sheriff," Maddie replied.

"I'm not worried about that. There could be trouble here. I need to check on it."

With that, he replaced his microphone and climbed up on the porch. He was about to step into the house when he heard a shuffling noise and reflexively spun back towards the clearing, drawing his gun and bringing his front sight into focus.

"Careful with that thing!" Millie shouted as she ducked. "Hold your fire!"

Dill lowered his revolver and gazed at Millie, whose bathrobe had fallen partially open. His lips turned crimson as she snatched her robe closed.

"Keep your eyes to yourself!" she snapped. "there's nothing here for you."

"We'll see about that, won't we," he said. It was a threat.

"What were you doing going into my house? You've got no business in there."

"I'm just doing my duty. We got a call about trouble out here. The door was open, and no one was around. I thought it best to check on things in case someone was sneaking around."

"You're the only one trespassing here. You're the one sneaking."

"Sneaking? Sneaking?" he said, mimicking Sméagol. "Not me. I'm sworn to serve and protect."

"Get out of my house!" she shouted.

"That's not very neighborly."

"Stuff your neighborly crap. I don't know you. You can talk to my husband when he goes to town. You're not welcome on this property unless we call you for help. Get out!"

"I heard you were a vixen. I look forward to seeing you again next time you swing into town."

"Get off our property. Now!" Millie yelled. "And don't come back. Ever."

Dill smiled and stepped off the porch. He kept his eyes on her as he got into his patrol car and started the engine.

"Next time I come up here, I'll have a warrant. I'll spend a lot of time with you then. On my terms."

Millie only glared at him and thought about Steven lying in the woods, bleeding out.

"Beat it, punk! You don't scare me," she said and pulled her shotgun out from under her robe. Her finger was on the trigger, and the muzzle slowly rose to the sheriff's head. "This is private property. No one will find your bones if you return for any reason."

Sheriff Dill suppressed a laugh and made an obscene gesture. He slammed his door, revved the engine twice to show what a man he was, and peeled out of the clearing like a high school sophomore, his brain zipped in his pants.

Millie didn't bother to watch him leave. The security system let her know when he cleared the property. She'd already jumped on their ATV and was heading back to her husband. She was reckless and nearly flipped the Tracker 800SX when she avoided a tree that had fallen near the trail. Composing herself, she chanted the phrase, "Slow is fast. Slow is fast."

When she pulled up next to Popoford, she saw that he hadn't moved since she'd left. Her heart sank, but she wasn't about to give up. She jumped out of the 800 as it was still coming to a stop and reached under his shoulders. She grabbed him under his armpits and dragged his dead weight to the Tracker.

She let him down and pressed a lever at the side of the cargo box. The box tilted up, making it easier for her to drag him into it. It took all her strength to hoist him high enough to finally flop him into the box, where she curled him up enough to almost fit.

Millie fought the fear that he had already died and hopped onto the 800. She rode home with more care than she had given in her race to return to him.

CHAPTER EIGHT

Popoford wasn't in Neverland. Nor was he one of Thursday Next's familiars. He thrashed about, fumbling to light in a suitable place, bouncing from one literary world to the next until he landed in the grey-scale starkness of a 1940s Noir nightmare. He lay cold, stretched out with a white sheet gently draping his naked body, waiting for the autopsy knife.

He tried to open his mouth to scream, but his jaw wouldn't move. Each effort he made to move any part of his body failed, and frustration swelled within him. He had to be alive. Otherwise, how could he hear the thumping in his chest? To begin with, how could there be thumping in his chest? How could he have these fantasies? He was startled, yet he remained immobile as someone pulled the sheet down, and the light increased through his closed lids.

"I'm here, Steven," Millie whispered.

Tears. He felt tears seeping from under his eyelids, and a burst of joy warmed him. He was alive!

"Open your eyes, darling," Millie said. "Come on. You can do it."

Popoford heard her voice, but it took a conscious effort and a few moments to get it done. The light blinded him, and he immediately squeezed his eyes shut again.

"Come on," Millie said, encouraging him. "Just open them slowly. Let yourself get used to the light. Okay? Slowly. That's it." She removed a handkerchief from her robe pocket and dabbed the corners of his eyes. Then she leaned closer and kissed him. "Welcome back, lover."

Popoford managed to strain a slight curl from his lips, and Millie took it for a grin.

"That's my man," she said and kissed him again. This time he didn't respond but fell into a shallow sleep.

She removed his clothes and threw them in a corner. Next, she inspected his wounds more closely and was astonished at what she found.

The contusion and hematoma swirls had faded rapidly. The impact wound was disappearing. The pale-green discoloration that had advanced up Popoford's right arterial artery had dissipated. He was no worse off than any man of his age and experience. It was a miracle, or a spell, for only God or the Devil could have accomplished this healing. Millie thought that if it had been God's work, then there was a miracle at hand. If it was the Devil's work, it was only a sleight of hand, a deception. She prayed for God's hand in the matter, but in her heart, she feared a return of the demon they had once fought, the man who had claimed to be her father: Simon Contlerust.

Millie dressed him in operationally ready fatigues and fashioned an empty cardboard box into a sled. Then, she lowered him from the bedroom closet into the tunnels that stretched under their driveway to the woods. Popoford had excavated the three-level tunnels long before Millie entered his life, and once again, they had come in handy.

She was so consumed with worry that her skills were inadequate she didn't notice Popoford was sitting up until his feet hit the floor. She turned at the sound, expecting to find him flopped in front of her. To her astonishment, he took two assured steps toward her and wrapped his arms around her, giving her a warm hug.

"I was sure I was dead," he said. "but here I am feeling great and ready to go."

Millie gently pushed him away and peered at him at arm's length.

"Are you alright? You should sit down. They almost killed you! Sit down, will you?"

"I'm okay. Millie. I've never felt better."

"That's not possible. How could you have recovered so fast?"

"Recovered from what?'

Millie was shocked. He was standing there with no indication of trauma. His skin was flush, like he'd just returned from a run. He looked to be in top shape. His eyes sparkled, and there was no evidence that any harm had come to him.

"You better sit down, Steven."

"Don't worry. I'm okay."

"How can you be? Just moments ago, I thought you were dead."

"I don't know. Who cares? I feel great now."

Millie just stared at him.

He gazed at her with a bemused expression. "I recover fast. If I felt bad, I'd tell you. Come on. Let's get upstairs. I'm hungry."

Millie was still staring at him when he reached for her and held her in his arms.

"Come on. Let's go," Popoford said. "You can tell me all about the sheriff while I scramble some eggs."

Millie's eyes popped. "How do you know about that? You were unconscious in the back of the ATV when that jerk showed up. How could you know?"

Popoford had a perplexed expression as he released her. "I don't know."

"What do you mean you don't know?"

"Just that. I can't remember anything after opening the front door except for a hazy image of a very short man. But I know the sheriff was here, and he threatened you."

Millie was amazed. She took his hand and led him to the stairs. He went up first, and they entered their bedroom through the trapdoor in their closet. Neither spoke until they sat at the kitchen table with a cup of coffee. It was Steven who broke the silence.

"Sarah's boy is learning to read," he said.

Millie's eyes widened. "Where did that come from? You need to tell me about how you know about the sheriff."

"I will, but I also know what the sheriff's up to."

"This is too weird," Millie said. "You must have a concussion. You haven't even seen the boy. And you weren't conscious when the sheriff was here. You imagine things."

Popoford put his face in his hands for a second. When he raised it again, he had a wild-eyed terror in his eye. "I don't know. Something is very wrong. I feel great but shouldn't. I know things I shouldn't know. I believe I can read the boy's mind. I know I can read yours and the sheriff's. This is not right. I don't know what's happened to me, but I'm scared."

Millie crossed herself. She reached out and held his face in her hands. "Me, too."

"Yes. I know! And you want to talk to Father Logan about it."

"How did you…Sorry," Millie paused in thought. Then she responded. "You knew…"

"Yes. Before you said it."

"…that I would say that."

She was dumbfounded. "How deep does it go?"

"So far," Popoford said, "no farther than what you think now. But I am getting hints of memories and internal arguments."

"And secrets?"

"Yes. Secrets that would be better left unspoken,"

Millie flushed and gave him a comforting smile. "For better or worse," she said.

CHAPTER NINE

Having taken the name and form of the little man, Contlerust, now known as Professor Shinkle, scrunched into the shape-shifted capsule that mimicked the slain scientist's body. The damned fiend sat in the highchair studying the green board and elegant formula chalked on it. He marveled at the beauty of the calligraphy itself and the sublime nature of its proof. He had solved the equation by probing the brain of the murdered genius who had concocted it. He used yellow chalk to differentiate the final solution. Once laid out, it appeared so apparent as to be inevitable. He thought such is the elegance of simplicity. The arrogant mind reduces poetic life to the prosaic.

Now he'd confirmed the formula's efficacy by injecting Popoford. His master plan, long fermenting in his mind, would now advance rapidly. Soon, all formed in God's image would happily transform into a layered, codified, and compliant cluster of willing tools scrambling to serve the Prince of the Earth.

After Contlerust had the real Professor Shinkle murdered, he'd called upon the lessor black angels of Hell to clear Section 33 of all clutter, repair the dilapidated fixtures, and rip out the many small offices to create one vast low-ceilinged cavern. Under-powered bulbs cast pools of weak light, fading into vast, bituminous voids.

He climbed down from the chair and began to walk. His gait straightened out a little more with each waddling step away from the green chalkboard. His countenance continued to alter as he passed through three pools of light. When he reappeared from the last black expanse and pushed the elevator button, his body was stretched to an average height, and his clothes were miraculously transformed to fit and flatter. He was no longer Professor Shinkle but the very private international financier and phantom Arthur Harcourt, proud founding member of the Globalist Nations United, GNU.

Harcourt straightened his tie and brushed his lapels as he stepped from the elevator.

He stood for a second on the roof of the thirty-three-story building for which the defunct clandestine agency, Section 33, was named. The prop wash of a Bell 525 Relentless helicopter ruffled his golden hair, and he put on a pair of sunglasses against the wind and the gleaming sun reflecting from the helo's sparkling red fuselage. A stylized scorpion, almost indistinguishable from the surrounding paint, was invisible save for those knowing where to look. International ID numbering was nonexistent, even though the helicopter was transported overseas when necessary.

Arthur Harcourt had walked the earth in many forms for centuries and in many guises. His international organization manipulated world financial markets and slipped its members and surrogates into lucrative advisory roles on boards of directors in global and local governments. They set up honey pots and cash funnels to ensnare the reluctant when they encountered resistance. The honorable and recalcitrant were shamed and defamed until they abandoned their principles. When resistance became annoying, kidnapping and murder of loved ones often did the trick. If it didn't, the stubborn stooge was deemed a write-off, and Harcourt would sink an ice pick to the hilt into his ear. Press, cops, coroners, lawyers, and judges made the legal mess disappear. The hogs sat safely, fat and happy. The straight-up shmucks who worked for a living and had nothing to offer the organization ultimately paid for the ride, but they never got a chance at the promised gold ring. Arthur Harcourt had other ways to corrupt their souls.

Harcourt climbed into the luxurious cabin of the Bell 525.

"Welcome aboard, Mister Harcourt."

"Thank you, Larry. Everything okay today."

"Shipshape, Sir. We should land in plenty of time for your appointment."

His disingenuous smile was imbued with deceit, appearing sincere. "Excellent, Larry. How's the family?"

Larry gave a thumbs up.

"How about you, John? Everything good at home?"

"As good as it gets," the co-pilot said."

"Good. Take it up, boys."

The 525's cabin had a custom layout. Instead of the standard sixteen passenger chairs, only four faced the middle area. When Harcourt took his seat, he pushed a button on his chair's console and a table scissored from the floor. He slid a panel aside, and a monitor rose into position. GNU's proprietary video conferencing app automatically loaded, and he was connected to his private secretary, Lindsey Cracker.

"Good morning, Sir."

"Good morning, Cracker. Give me the headlines."

"Yes, Sir. Our universities are in the news for stipulating that all their undergraduates must volunteer for military duty if they have no plans for advanced degrees and wish to complete their undergraduate education. Our press is hailing it as a sign of patriotism returning to the hallowed halls."

Cracker noticed the sneer on Harcourt's mouth and smiled to himself. "Corporate's mandate to ramp up rare earth exploration in Afghanistan got a big boost when your protégé, Sid Melton, put his Department of Defense seal of approval on a joint venture between Signal Metals & Munitions and the Chinese Communist Party. Of course, Pakistan will cover for our direct involvement, and China will deny all knowledge.

"Our friends on both sides of the aisle and the various agencies will blame those who oppose us. The press has its talking points and red herrings ready for the "Go" signal.

"It's not my place, I know," Cracker concluded, "but I think our friends and associates have done a wonderful job, Mister Harcourt."

Harcourt's sneer deepened as he spoke. "They're only doing what they want to do. I offered them the juiciest prize they could imagine, and they may get it. Or maybe they'll just yearn for it throughout eternity with no hope of satisfaction. They made their deals and bought their verdicts. They gave their souls away. It's such an expected choice that it surprises me when someone says no."

Cracker nodded without another word.

"Have the principals assembled. I will be in the conference room in exactly sixty-eight minutes."

CHAPTER TEN

Merced was hot even in the shade. Weather Underground predicted clear skies, but the sun wasn't shining even at noon. Soot rained steadily upon Sarah Tufftang as she hurried from Raley's to her car. Her three-month-old boy was strapped to her back and had two masks covering his face. It wasn't Covid she feared; it was smoke poisoning. The forests, mismanaged by government mandate, had been bone dry for many summers.

Infected with beetles, burdened with excess trees, and cluttered with twigs, leaves, and dead branches, they were susceptible to fire, and many acres were burning out of control for a fourth consecutive season. Hospitals were cluttered with poor souls struggling to breathe. And those who managed to keep their lungs healthy stayed inside with air conditioning blowing twenty-four hours a day except when rolling blackouts left them to sweat it out.

Sarah wasn't worried about what the soot would do to her. Her concerns centered on the boy, his phenomenal size, and her aching back. He grew, and she coughed. He grew, and she lost weight. He grew, and now at three months old, he was talking up a storm like a three-year-old. Her son was beginning to scare her, especially when she caught him gazing at her, a queer, penetrating coolness in his eyes. The occurrences were becoming more common, and each time they happened, she expected him to flinch first. But she always lost the staring contest.

There was no doubt that the boy was brilliant. Each day gave proof that he was exceptional. When she had him strapped securely in his safety seat, he pulled his thumb out of his mouth and shocked her.

"Mommy, your friend, Steven, wants to say hello."

Sarah froze. "What did you say, Gabby?"

"Steven and Millie want to talk to you."

Sarah shivered. Her blood seemed to drain from her head. Cold sweat formed on her temples, and she reached for her Miraculous Medal, crushing it in her grip. Blood seeped onto her palms and flowed to her wrists. She was in shock and felt nothing but horror.

"Don't be afraid, Mommy. I've been talking to them in my head just like I do with you."

Sarah nearly fainted as she stammered. "Like…you do…with me?"

Gabriel Singleton Tufftang cocked his head a little as a loveable smile crossed his lips, and Sarah heard his voice whispering in her head. "Mommy, you love me so much, and I love you. You know it's me. I know you do, and so do you. You know."

"What are you? Who are you?"

"Your son,"

"But what are you?"

"A messenger."

"From whom?"

"You already know."

"I'm afraid,"

"Be accepting."

"How?"

"Ask your Virgin Mother."

Sarah broke down into tears. "Why me?"

"God has chosen you."

"Is Simon your father?" Millie asked.

"My father is in heaven. He momentarily put my spirit into Simon's so you wouldn't bear a son of Satan."

"I'm not worthy,"

"How can you judge?"

"Tell me."

"Am I here?"

"Yes."

"Then you are worthy. Be silent and always listen closely. Much will be revealed to you, and much will be asked of you."

"It sounds so hard,"

"He is with you. Do not be afraid."

Sarah didn't know how she got home. She was standing in the kitchen with a pile of totes on her counter. The groceries were not there.

She remembered getting into her car and trussing Gabe into his car seat, but that was it. The in-between was blank.

She opened her refrigerator and tentatively peeked inside. The beer she'd bought was on the top shelf, so she propped the door wider and inventoried shelf-by-shelf, drawer-by-drawer until she was convinced each and everything on her list had already been put away.

Gabe was in his highchair, concentrating on the dozen Cheerios in his bowl. He could move groceries from their bags and into a refrigerator. That was simply mind over matter. But his precision motor skills were lagging behind his mental capacity, yet he wasn't concerned. His muscles and flesh weren't his concern, and his mind was developing rapidly and on schedule.

CHAPTER ELEVEN

The collapse of the prior malevolent organization, The Supreme Five, in ancient Greek, "*to anótato pénte,*" or TAPalong with the death of his lackeys and three of his lieutenants, was nothing but a noxious splat he might step in while walking down a city sidewalk. Life was nothing in the entirety of time, and operations sometimes failed. Having fallen from heaven with his Master in the great rebellion, Contlerust had been seasoned by centuries of constant combat. TAP had failed. So what? He had other operations whose gears spun smoothly. Globalist Nations United was the lynchpin that secured his malevolent international corruption while ancillary organizations of divergent political makeup spread his poison deep into all world societies. For men are sinners, and many never repent. So many sinners are eager to earn a place in Hell. So many fools at his beck and call. It was almost too easy.

As Contlerust, now calling himself Arthur Harcourt, entered the board room of GNU, he greeted all the attendees but gave a special nod to two of them, for they were his confidants. Under the flesh, they were his doppelgangers. It was Contlerust who inhabited each body. Harcourt, the slim woman, and the muscular man were Contlerust himself. And each was determined to uncover any plot by the others to bring Contlerust into disfavor with their Master. Every board member was a demon bent on toppling Harcourt. But none knew that Harcourt harbored a desire to dethrone the Prince of the Earth, Satan.

Harcourt sat at the head of the table and called the meeting to order with a brief but decisive speech.

"Whatever you are working on, put it in an underling's hands. Clear your calendars. I am here to report on a scientific discovery that will bring us outright control of every region, every country, and person on Earth."

The members of his Board of Directors murmured to each other.

"Silence! Keep your opinions to yourselves. There will be no vote on the initiative I am instituting. No discussion. No alternative. You will comply and succeed or suffer the wrath you deserve. Am I understood?"

The slim woman asked a question because Contlerust had put it in her head.

"Why must we end our projects? Mine is nearly complete. Success is at hand."

Contlerust glared at her and outstretched his arm, clenching his hand in a strangling grip. Without touching her, she began to gag.

"Is my answer clear?" he asked, and she nodded.

He released his grip and stroked his own throat, for what was hers was his. They were one. The muscular man released a sympathetic cough.

"Are there further questions?" he said and went on without a pause. "Good. Unbeknownst to you, I have appropriated a means to accelerate the Master's grand plan. A sequence of events will be implemented whereby the world's entire population will be joined as one mind and controlled exclusively by me. To begin with, core individuals will have a genetic worm implanted in their bloodstream. This worm will tunnel deep within their brains, harvesting every detail of their intelligence: memories, capabilities, loyalties, contacts, and desires. It is a rapid sequence and can complete its tasks within an hour. Once the sequence reaches a critical threshold, each subject's mind will connect to the minds of people in their sphere of influence no matter how shallow their connection may be."

Contlerust paused and sipped some water while telepathically scanning his Board of Directors. He had self-injected the worm while on the Bell 525 helicopter flight.

"And once connected," he continued, "the desire for the worm will be seeded in their friends and casual acquaintances alike. Soon, a lust to belong will overpower their will. They will demand to be included in the collective. It will be a self-expanding swarm where governments fulfill their dreams of total control by harvesting everyone's cognitive data and assigning careers and futures to each person based on the master's needs. Every person on Earth will obtain their true capabilities. Every human will become an efficient drone in the service of our Master. All desire to better oneself will end because each person will be in their proper place. We will extinguish their God, and our Master will rule over them. The age of hope is dying. The age of despair is on the rise. We will improve mankind for the pleasure of the Master and his favored ones."

The board members sat quietly. Stunned. They dared not say a word. But eventually, devilish smiles slowly contorted their faces. Seeing this and reading their minds, Contlerust was pleased. There would be no rebellion today.

"This meeting is ended," he said, but his pronouncement did not move any of them. He closed his eyes and felt the lust in their black spirits. None there was blacker than his, yet he fed on the hate and deceit flowing from them and relished its bitter taste.

He whispered a sort of prayer. "Master, I have delivered for you. I am yours."

Much to his surprise, a stifling yellow brimstone fog filled the room, and a rumbling voice so deep that it was barely heard rattled the entire building.

"I know your intentions. Your lust is dangerous and unbecoming."

Contlerust shuddered. A profound silence followed while the fog slowly lifted.

CHAPTER TWELVE

Sheriff Dill woke up on Tuesday with an ocular seizure. Zigzag lightning scurried along a half-moon trail on the upper-right edge of his vision. He noticed it first when he realized he had a peripheral blind spot. He tried his regular treatment: two Advil and a few minutes relaxing in a dark room, but after a half-hour, the electric storm had increased, and a migraine was sinking its fangs into his occipital lobe. He rose in a frenzied panic, sweating and groaning from the increasing pain. He grew hysterical with confusion. He was alone in his upstairs apartment, claustrophobic and wild to get out, crazed to make the pain stop. In his madness, he went into the bathroom, feeling his way as his eyesight continued to fail. Soon he found himself in the bathtub pressing his forehead against the cool wall tiles. It felt good but didn't fix anything. When he saw the small window high on the wall, he fumbled with it until he clawed it open. He had just removed the screen and was trying to crawl through the small opening when his front door swung open, and his landlord rushed into the apartment.

"What are you doing? Come on, get down from there. That's it. Come on."

His landlord helped him shuffle out of the bathroom and onto his bed, where he collapsed and passed out.

Several hours later, Dill was sitting up. His landlord sat quietly in a chair across the room. There was a bowl with water and a damp washcloth within reach, and Dill pressed it against his head and eyes. The headache was nearly gone, and his eyes were back to normal, but as he stood, he knew something was wrong. He felt wobbly, unsteady on his feet and in his mind. His thoughts were skidding from here to there without purpose. It was all blank when he tried to remember what had happened that morning and the day before. He'd never had such problems. Now headaches, blindness, and screwy thoughts were followed by an encore of amnesia. What the hell was happening?

Sheriff Dill's landlord was named Joseph. He went by Effie. He'd never seen Dill like this before, and he'd known him for a couple of years. Dill had stepped in and calmed the locals down when Sheriff Florter was killed. Most folks in town thought him a good and steady man, well respected by all. Effie was still at Dill's side when he finally came out of his stupor and said something.

"Where have I been, Effie?"

"I found you right here in your apartment yelling for help. It took a bit of coaxing to get you to stop climbing the walls. I got you into bed, and now you're awake. That's all I know."

"But did you see me coming home?"

"I saw your patrol car coming up the drive, but I didn't pay any attention."

"And I didn't tell you where I'd been?"

"No. Why should you? You always keep your business to yourself. It's not for me to ask you where you've been."

"That's too bad, Effie, 'cause I'd like to know myself," Dill said.

Effie was sitting in a straight-backed chair by the window. He was about to speak, but shut his mouth, got up, and walked to the door. "My advice, Sheriff, is to get some more rest. You need to get your head on straight. If anyone comes around looking for you, send them away."

Sheriff Dill didn't hear Effie's last words. He was already passed out and was ensnared in a deranged dream acting the creep hellbent on rape. His quarry was half-dressed, just stepping out of the forest. She was a feisty one armed with a shotgun. They had words he had forgotten as soon as he thought them, for the dream was over when Effie started to shake him out of his stupor.

"Wake up, Sheriff! Come on! Get up! There's a man here looking for you, and he's got a woman with him. She's got a shotgun, and he's got a mean scowl on his face. You want me to tell them you're not here?"

Dill thought for a second and shook his head. "Let them come up. I've seen them before."

Effie shook his head but did as the sheriff said. He walked down the driveway and told Popoford and Millie to go up to the Sheriff's apartment. Then he hurried into his own apartment and dialed 911.

Dill was standing at his bedroom door. The headache was nearly gone, and he could see clearly, more clearly than he ever had. "Come in, Steven. You won't need that shotgun, Millie. My service pistol's on the counter. I'm not about to go for it. Come in and sit down. I think Steven and I have a great deal to talk about. Let's start with an apology. I'm going crazy. What I did wasn't me. It couldn't have been. You know that, don't you, Steven? You know what happened because you know what I'm thinking. Just like I know what you're thinking. Tell me what's happening. Please tell me."

Popoford kept his pistol in his shoulder holster and gestured for Millie to lower her gun. Stepping into the apartment, they split up as best they could: Millie stood by the door, and Popoford took a seat in a chair across from the couch where Dill was seated.

"Why is this happening?" Popoford asked, and Dill shrugged.

"I don't know. I can read your thoughts. You can read mine. How and why is beyond me."

Popoford nodded. He knew that Dill was telling the truth. "I don't know you very well, Sheriff, so why don't you tell me what's been going on? I know you've had a headache and are confused. I know how you behaved up at the cabin. What I need to know is what happened before we were connected. What made you act the way you did?"

Sheriff Dill rubbed his temples and took a long drink of water. He seemed to be staring at nothing, but his eyes moved as if seeing an object in motion.

"What is it, Sheriff?" Popoford asked. "What do you see?"

"I'm fuzzy. I've had a horrible headache, and I'm having difficulty getting my thoughts in order."

Popoford just glanced at him, but Millie offered consolation. "Migraines make me crazy," she said without relaxing her grip on her shotgun.

"Crazy. Whacky. I don't know," Dill said, "but it's hard to remember how it started."

"Do you remember getting out of bed this morning?"

The sheriff rubbed his temples and draped a wet washcloth over his head. "Well, I got up early. The sun was coming through the window, and I couldn't sleep. It was so bright."

Popoford was losing patience and showed Millie his frustration.

"Can you get to the point, Langley?" she said congenially. "It's important."

"I heard a voice coming from the light."

"You mean the window, right?" Popoford said.

"No. The light. No one was there, but the voice was warm, golden, bright, like the sun."

Popoford and Millie exchanged glances in silence.

"It sounds crazy, doesn't it?" Dill said.

"Not to us," Millie answered. "We've had a rough morning, too, especially when you tried to get in our house."

Sheriff Dill pushed the washcloth away from his eyes. He was astonished. "What is this, some kind of shakedown? This is the first time I've been up on your property. You know that. Anyway, it's my policy to enter a house only when the owner or the law says I can. You haven't known me long, but at least you must know I have a reputation for following the law. I made that clear when I first got to Whimsy."

Millie didn't wait for Popoford to defend her. "Did you ever say you'd avoid making nasty advances on married women?"

Dill was dumbfounded. His jaw hung slack, and his eyes ached so much he felt like they were about to bleed.

"Don't tell me you don't remember that," Millie said.

Dill's mouth hung open. There was nothing to say.

It was Popoford who broke the spell. "He doesn't remember a thing, Millie. After the voice told him what to do, he became its slave. His memory had been wiped clean until he woke up with a splitting headache. I can imagine what happened, but all evidence would have been wiped clean by now."

They sat in the room in silence until Sheriff Dill spoke up. "I had a bad dream before the headache got me."

"Yes," Popoford said. "It was the dwarf, wasn't it?"

"How did you know that?" Sheriff Dill said.

"You mean you don't know what the dwarf did to Steven?"

"No. How could I?"

Popoford raised his hand to stop Millie from continuing. "I think he's had enough pressure for one day, Millie. Let's let him rest."

Millie caught on right away. Sheriff Dill's two-way telepathic ability was spotty. The dwarf or someone else was selective about mindreading. Popoford, Millie, and the Sheriff had been trapped in their parts, and madness was the play's common theme.

They sat quietly for a few minutes, Millie listening to Popoford, Popoford listening to Millie and Dill, and Dill struggling to regain cohesive thoughts of any kind.

Suddenly, a thunderous shockwave rattled the apartment building.

"Earthquake!" Popoford shouted as he grabbed Millie's arm and pulled her close. Sheriff Dill sat up stiff in his chair as a cloud snuffed out the morning sun, and a leaden sky transformed the early morning into a false gloaming. A pervasive silence dominated the air. Popoford ordered Dill to hit the floor, but his words went nowhere, as if soundwaves were stuck in glue.

Panic rose in their hearts as they bunched up on the floor, afraid that the world's end was upon them.

Dill opened his mouth in a red-faced silent bellow, and Popoford retched at the terror he could feel in the sheriff's head. Millie calmed him down as she silently prayed her favorite prayer, the Memorare, earnestly repeating her plea even as Popoford joined in. Together, they calmed down as they relaxed. Sheriff Dill felt a new peace. But as Popoford began to stand, a croaking voice spoke to him alone.

"Oh, poor Steven, your little house is a pile of ash, your forest kindling, your tunnels collapsed. Pledge yourself to me, and I will make you a collector of souls. You will feast on the insipid and rule over millions. Join me on the dais of honor. Come, Steven. Leave this weary world behind. Come to me, you who are heavily laden, and I shall give you all the wondrous things your dreams are made of."

Popoford felt exhausted, weak, and drained. He wanted to die, even an eternal dying, a dying without end, without peace.

It was Millie's voice in his head that finally broke through the spell.

"Steven! Listen to me! Look at me! Now! Look!"

He focused on her and realized that though her mouth was moving, the sound he heard wasn't her voice carrying to him. Her telepathic words were in his head.

"Steven! Stand up! Grab the sheriff, and let's get out of here. If our place is gone, we'll start again. We must get back there and protect it if it's a lie. Steven! Let's go!"

CHAPTER THIRTEEN

The Sun was still obscured as Popoford drove his car onto his access road. Sheriff Dill was in the front seat, and Millie was in the back with her gun ready if the sheriff turned on them. She couldn't read his mind and didn't trust him at all. They pulled into the clearing and were amazed to see their little home standing intact. One glance at the woods put the lie to its reported incineration. All appeared peaceful, yet an eerie silence smothered that illusion when they parked and stepped out onto the gravel. No birds were warbling; no breeze rustled the leaves, no insects chirped in the still air, for the silence of death hovered over the land, and all was in shadow.

They all stood still for several minutes, desperately seeking comfort in any slight sound that might confirm life. The sound that came did not soothe. It rattled their souls to the core.

As if a hundred famished lion prides had gathered around them in the woods and on the cliff ridge behind the house, a snarl, at first only a whisper, steadily grew into a thundering, growling roar. The earth beneath the telepathic trio loosened and was set in motion by the sine wave's subsonic vibration. It pulsated with auditory power; the forest, the clearing, and the house rolled in increasing swells until the crest was six feet high, its trough six feet deep. Up and down the earth thrust with unnatural exaggeration. Even though the ferocity of the cycling wave and the tremendous roar of the enraged lions were terrifying, as the quake gradually subsided, it became rhythmically tranquilizing. Popoford, Millie, and Dill, with heads bowed, were relieved though not without fear by the time the earth stood still.

Millie scanned the woods seeking evidence of danger, yet beyond the curtain of trees, there was no sign of dwarf or beast.

Popoford turned back to their house and was amazed to see it still sitting as it had been, unscathed. The cliff was still intact.

The sounds of nature returned as if having never departed. But above the charming calls of woodland creatures came a distant howl, a predatory warning from the Dark Angel's emissary, the shapeshifter of many names, the dwarf.

Popoford not only heard the howl but the message as well. And Millie shuddered as she overheard it in her head.

"You are warned, Steven. You cannot escape the power of the Master. You will obey his will. You will become what he wishes you to become."

Popoford couldn't help himself. Recognizing that the fantastic illusion had caused no damage, he broke out in a bellowing laugh. "Your poison has no sting! Death is your Master, and he knows he's beaten."

Time ticked only two mortal seconds when an unearthly scream rose in the wilderness. Sheriff Dill doubled over into a fetal ball, shuddering as his last breath ran dry. He lay still, his eyes bulging and blood trickling from his mouth.

"Your dear Millie will be next, Steven, but I'll take my time with her."

Millie and Popoford gazed in terror into each other's eyes. They heard each other praying for the Blessed Virgin's help as Millie prepared to die.

"Silence!" the demon howled. "Silence!"

But the newlyweds continued their supplication, and the dwarf demon went silent that day.

They knew he would return, but they also knew they had the best defense in the world, and that was the offense of Mary and her Holy Legions.

They went to Sheriff Dill's body and stretched him out on the gravel; they continued their call for divine protection by invoking St. Michael, the Archangel's defense in battle. They were firm in their belief that Satan may have shown his power but that they must never weaken.

"Millie! Let's get him inside! We might be able to save him!"

Millie had heard his thoughts before Popoford spoke and ran into the house as Popoford bent over the sheriff.

Dill was delirious, floundering on the gravel, a shredded man susceptible to any illusion. The remnants of his migraine had mixed with the hallucination and compounded its effect.

Millie raced back to Sheriff Dill, dropped to her knees, and applied a cold compress. She made him sip from a water bottle, and in minutes Dill was sitting upright; his bleeding stopped. Emergency crews hurried up the twisting mountain road to the Popoford residence with their ambulance's pulsing wail and a fire truck's shrieking siren running interference.

CHAPTER FOURTEEN

Popoford and Millie were resting on their bed, with Dill on the couch in the front room. It was early afternoon and the EMTs and sheriff's men, being the last to roll down the long gravel road on their way back to Whimsy, made slow progress as they followed the firetruck through the mountain curves. It was a glorious day with the fresh breeze swirling sweet woodland perfumes and musty loam fragrances about the clearing. When the sun was dipping behind the treetops, Dill wandered out the front door and sat on the porch with his feet touching the ground.

The sheriff wasn't stupid, but he felt like he was. He wasn't a jerk, but he knew he had been. He wasn't dead, but he might have been. He wasn't sure about what had happened from the day before the onset of his migraine to the earthquake and his remarkable recovery, but he knew there was some bizarre shit going on. And he was smack-dab in the middle of it.

The next day, Millie got up as dawn came. Popoford had been awake for hours just lying in bed, thinking. He reached out for her, but she was already heading into the kitchen and didn't notice. He watched her go and returned to his thoughts.

They were as dark as devilish thoughts could be, and he shuddered and tried to drive them from his mind without success. His memory was scant, his imagination ripe as he considered the meaning of recent events.

Contlerust had returned. It appeared that he wanted them to live. He could have killed Popoford with the injection or all of them with the earthquake illusion. They were the mice and he, the cat. But was he only tormenting them? If so, Popoford expected the game to bore the demon very soon. Certainly, Contlerust had a more malevolent purpose in mind. But what could it be?

Popoford grew tired of stewing on the possibilities and got out of bed. He quickly dressed and walked to the kitchen. Millie and Sheriff Dill were sitting at the table drinking coffee.

"Good morning," Millie said as she stood.

She kissed him and poured him a cup. They sat together in silence for a minute. Then all at once, Popoford and Dill spoke the exact words in unison.

"I'm waiting for instructions."

Millie had overheard the other side of the conversation in Popoford's mind. It was a simple question.

"What are you doing?"

Then she heard, "The implanted tissue has melded into your neuro system and has completed its crawl through your neurons. All your capabilities have been inventoried and the results transmitted to GNU systems. You are relegated to the cluster where your ability will be of most service to the world. You will serve where and when you are needed."

Millie reached out and shook Popoford's shoulder.

"Wake up, Steven. What was that voice? Who was it?"

It was Dill who answered. "It's our leader, Fr. Finch."

"What do you mean? What leader? Is he the head of the Sheriff's union?"

Popoford raised his hand to cut Dill off. "Let's not have this conversation right now," he said with a knowing glance at Millie. "I need to lay this situation out for you myself. Just you and me. Okay?"

Millie frowned. She'd overheard the conversation through Popoford's mind and knew everything already.

Popoford, hearing her thoughts, shook his head. "The sheriff is on another wavelength. Keep it to yourself for now. Please."

Sheriff Dill was still groggy, and his memory was fuzzy. He felt exceptionally thirsty and gulped all his coffee before looking around the table. When his eyes finally focused, they landed on Millie, who was staring at him in return.

"How're you feeling?" she said. "Yesterday was rough. Maybe you should lie down again. You know, we thought you were dead out there."

"I'm just fine," he said, but his distant stare suggested otherwise.

"Langley," Popoford said. "You need to take it easy. With us coming in hot about your treatment of Millie, how you tried to bust into our house, and the earthquake, you really need a rest."

Sheriff Dill sat still and didn't respond.

Popoford looked at him and read his mind. A change had come over the sheriff. Popoford knew all about it since he had experienced much of what Dill was going through.

"Tell me your orders," Popoford said. Dill blinked twice and divulged all he knew.

"I'm to report to you, Sir. You're next in the chain of command. I'm an observer meant to go about my life as I always have. But I will send you a private message if something comes up."

"Excellent, Sheriff," Popoford said like he was the boss. "You were handpicked for your loyalty. I will contact you when you are needed. Have another cup of coffee, and we'll take you back to town in a little bit. In the meantime, stay at the table and wait for us to return. And cut the cord to my communications. Understand?"

Sheriff Dill, big and powerful as his body was, wore a face and attitude of a servant. He was no sycophant, but he was attentive and ready to please. Popoford could see it in his eyes and hear it in his rattled brain.

"Come on, Millie. Let's take a walk."

Popoford and Millie stepped onto their porch, walking across the clearing and into the woods. He held her hand but kept silent as they walked a few yards deeper into the trees. They stopped, and Popoford placed his hand on an earthen mound. He found the handle and opened the hidden hatch to the underground tunnels. As Millie entered, he moved aside and cast an experienced eye about the surrounding forest. Then he entered the tunnel himself and closed the door.

"Steven," Millie said, but he put his finger to her lips, asking for silence.

He flipped on the lights and quietly led the way until they came to a door he opened. Once again, he cautioned silence and directed Millie to descend the stairs that led two stories below. He killed the lights in the upper tunnel and closed the door, locking it from the inside.

They passed the first lower level and continued to descend until they reached the bottom of the stairwell. In a few more steps, they got to the wall where a massive safe door was hung. Popoford keyed in his combination. He spun the vault's handle, letting the thick, heavy, precisely balanced door swing smoothly inward. Only when he'd closed the door behind them did he begin to talk.

"I designed the walls of this safe and did the construction myself, just like all the work in the tunnels. You know all that. But I recently made improvements to the safe."

"Like what," Millie said.

"Like incorporating Chameleon Ultrasonic voice recorder jammers to eliminate the possibility of eavesdropping. Like installing oxygen-production systems that are guaranteed to last a hundred years. Like extending the chamber into an underground greenhouse equipped with internal sunlight naturally delivered by redundant systems of flexible light-transmitting rods. Water comes from natural aquifers, streaming freshwater through underground channels throughout the eastern Sierra slopes. There's a refrigeration room accessible through one of the other safes lining that interior. The food supply can last for two hundred years if one is a miser, a shorter life if one cherishes good food. In short, we could stay here until we die if we had to. What do you say to that?"

"No, thank you."

"You're serious," Popoford said without expression.

"Darn right! Who wants to live like that? I'd go crazy stowed away below decks until we die. It's like being buried alive!"

Popoford smiled, and it seemed to irritate Millie even more.

"Why are you laughing at me."

"I'm not," Popoford said, breaking into laughter. "I hate the idea, too. I'm letting you know that we can talk down here without being heard. I'm not planning to squat here until I die."

"But your thoughts can be heard."

"Only by you. This structure protects our thoughts."

"How do you know that? That's not possible," Millie said, her face taut with anxiety.

Popoford took her in his arms and nuzzled her throat. "I know it because I can't communicate with whoever spoke to my mind when we were upstairs."

"You mean what happened with you and Sheriff Dill? That Fr. Finch crap?"

"That's it," Popoford said. "Fr. Finch can't hear me while I'm down here."

Millie looked at him like he was nuts.

"Millie, it means we will always have a place to go if things get rough. It means we can talk right now about what we're up against. It means we can steal away from time to time like we were husband and wife."

"We are husband and wife," she said. "We don't need to steal away."

"Perhaps you'll reconsider when you realize that Fr. Finch would essentially be a third person in our nuptial bed. I'm not going for that. Are you?"

Millie pulled away from him and looked him straight in the eyes.

"I didn't think of that. Fr. Finch can experience everything you can?"

"I'm assuming the answer is yes until I know better."

Millie turned away from him and walked deeper into the room. When she was ready to speak again, she turned around; her jaw set, her eyes shining cold as steel.

"That's not happening on my watch, Mr. Popoford. Not ever. You need to do something about this."

"Like what?" Popoford said.

"Like get upstairs and bring our bed down here!"

Popoford was under no illusion that his third-level subterranean vault was a secret.

First, Contlerust had known about it and promised to return one day to confiscate the munitions Popoford had collected there.

Second, Popoford had thought about what he was doing not only as he led Millie to the vault but before when he was examining Sheriff Dill's thrashing body. If he thought something, it seemed inevitable that this leader, Fr. Finch, to whom Dill was reporting and whoever was causing the hallucinations, also knew his thoughts. All he could do was plan his defenses well enough to keep himself and Millie safe.

Millie looked over her shoulder as she stepped through their escape hatch hidden in their bedroom closet. "I don't intend to stay down there forever. We've lots to do. I'm getting a strong signal from Sarah. I'm going to call her."

CHAPTER FIFTEEN

Contlerust, in one of his many guises, sat at the witness table in the Capitol building, answering the questions of the chairman of the House Subcommittee on Human Advancement. He wore the black cassock and white collar of a Catholic priest in mockery of the Universal Church. He smiled at his little joke, for today he would send Catholic norms into a downward spiral only the Devil himself could fully appreciate.

Fr. Finch, as he called himself, was about to testify to the acceptability of transhumanism within the Catholic Church's dogma. His comments would carry the great weight of Papal Authority as a purported Jesuit scholar and emissary of the Pope.

What he would attest to this day would rock the Christian world and spectacularly defame the Church. When he finished today's hit job, he would emerge as the great Satan of Rome and the great Savior of secular reformation. He would argue that God's plan had thwarted man, markedly reducing humans, leaving them unsuitable to inherit the earth, let alone the solar system. Fr. Finch would declare that it is time to augment man with the tools that God, in his unquestioned wisdom, had provided the scientists and the top progressive thinkers of the unfolding age. Artificial means propelling man's limited intelligence beyond its present state must be embraced, fostered, and funded internationally. America must lead the way to transhumanism by employing the technosphere. Those who object must be silenced in the name of the Lord!

"The Committee will come to Order." The gavel struck the chairman's sounding block in a lackadaisical and pendulous motion mimicking the ennui in her voice. "Order. Order. The House will come to order." There was no hint of exclamation in her delivery. She appeared bored out of her mind, but her mask of indifference could never reveal her psychological state.

As the legislative body finally settled in for what they expected to be a dull morning session, the TV cameras swung from the subcommittee Chairman to the congressmen. They were sorting their notes in preparation for their testimony and the subsequent examination expected from the opposition party. The priest sat calmly, his eyes at half-mast, focused on the beyond. His composed expression sharply contrasted with the harried look of the other witnesses. Seated between them, he had claimed center stage and the theatrical assumption that his voice represented primary truth.

Fr. Finch had reason to be calm. He had been assured that what he said today would become the foundational rationale for future legislation. It was his Master that had assured him. And the same being that owned him also owned the Chairman and most of her party. The fix was in.

The three witnesses had delivered their written statements well before the deadline. They'd been working on them for weeks and were well-prepped for questioning.

One of the women was from the ad hoc citizen's Committee on the Sanctity of Life.

The other claimed to speak for the Creatures of the Woods, a one-woman crusade in defiance of forest management.

The priest represented a rising portion of the Catholic Church whose notions purportedly came directly from The Holy Spirit in response to stodgy Dogma, outmoded in these enlightened times, requiring reason to propel the faith forward beyond centuries of backward thinking in which Rome indulged.

Fr. Finch carried the portfolio of an obscure Argentinean priest on a mission to the United Nations. His wallet was lighter but still abundantly full following a whirl-wind week of meetings with international grifters and national press luminaries with similar credentials. His persuasive skill was becoming well known in the halls of Congress, and several of the committee's representatives were anxious to make straight the path of today's proposed legislation.

"The House Subcommittee on Human Advancement will come to Order!" the chairman repeated loudly with a crash of her gavel as if she meant it.

Five minutes later, the last of the recalcitrant committee members took their seats. Some opened their folders to look at the written testimony for the first time; some ignored it altogether. Others gave a knowing nod to the witnesses. Two, Uwibajije from Washington and Skelton from Texas, made sure their prepared questions were ready for the struggle ahead.

The Chairman, Representative Clampshell from Seattle, opened the proceedings with her comments on transhumanism and the singularity where man and machine become one by defining terms her staff had researched. Thank goodness for them because she had no idea what any of the day's issue was about. All she knew was that the votes needed to move forward with funding had already been secured. Funding was a cinch. The hearing was an unnecessary evil.

"Having read all the most recent results of multiple studies on the subject at hand," she concluded, "there is no doubt in my mind that this committee will quickly advise the committee of the whole to move swiftly in funding this vital work. Our enemies are undoubtedly on course to beat us to the prize.

"Now, the witnesses may proceed with their testimony. Will the first witness state your name and expertise in the matter? Father, if you please."

Fr. Finch leaned slightly into the microphone. "If it pleases Madam Chairwoman, I ask that the ladies at the table be provided the courtesy of going first." His smile was broad and genuine. He wanted them to put their mushy ideas on display for all the world to scorn so he could relegate them to bumpkins with his testimony's first sentence.

"Very well," Representative Clampshell said. "We admire your chivalry, Father. Ms. Spearwuts, please state your full name and your expertise in the matter at hand."

The subcommittee members' minds began wandering.

CHAPTER SIXTEEN

The phone rang and rang. Millie finally hung up, but she tried again, and Sarah answered on the first ring.

"Hello?"

"Sarah! It's me! I've been thinking about you forever."

"Millie, I'm so sorry I missed your wedding. Things have been crazy here with little Gabe. He's a handful. Too smart for his own good."

Millie laughed. "Proud Mom, huh?"

"Yeah, but it's been hard. He's more than a handful."

"I can imagine," Millie replied.

Sarah didn't answer.

"Did I say something that hurt your feelings?" Millie asked.

Sarah took a deep breath before answering. "No. It's just that I feel so alone sometimes. Gabe is unusual. He's a large boy and a special child."

"Oh, Sarah, I had no idea. I feel for you."

Once again, Sarah took her time before answering. "Millie, I believe that you and I have the same belief that all children are a gift from God. No matter what He provides, it's nothing we can't handle. What God has given me is far beyond any expectation. My boy Gabe can read my mind, and I can read his."

The gasp at the other end of the line didn't surprise Sarah; what Millie said floored her.

"Of course, he's Simon's son. I should have expected it." Millie regretted her words even as she spoke them.

"What do you mean? How could you know anything about this?" Sarah exclaimed and, suddenly regretting her outburst, tried to cover her error. "I mean, how can you know anything about what I'm going through?"

Millie didn't hold back. "Because it's happening here, too! I never told you about how Simon died, but I think it's about time you heard the truth."

"What do you mean? Do you know how your father died?" Sarah asked. "If you do, why haven't you told me? I thought we were friends."

There was silence on the line as they both listened to the other's accelerated breathing on the other end of the call.

Millie finally answered with cautiously metered words.

"He was swallowed up in an earthquake. He just vanished as the fissure closed."

Sarah gasped. "Were you there?"

"Yes."

"Tell me what happened. I need to know."

When Millie spoke again, dark tones mingled with sadness and fear.

"All I'll say now is that it was a fitting end. To tell you the whole story without being with you would be impossible. I have to see you, so you'll know I'm telling the truth. You need to see my face to believe my story."

"That's not possible, now. I'm having a difficult time just managing classes and handling Gabe. There's no way I can travel now."

Millie could hear Gabe crying in the background.

"I can come to you, Sarah."

"But you were just married a couple of days ago. You can't leave Steven now."

"You needn't worry about that. We have our own mind-reading act we're working on."

"That's funny, I guess," Sarah said, surprised by Millie's reference to mind reading.

"Not so much, Sarah. It is what it is. I'll get on the road tomorrow or soon after that. I'll let you know when I'm leaving."

"Millie?"

"Yes."

"Thank you," Sarah said.

"Thank me or hate me but wait until I tell you the whole story before you thank me again. I'll call you back soon."

CHAPTER SEVENTEEN

The first witness to present the summary of her testimony before the House Subcommittee on Human Advancement was a pretty farm girl who was far too young to give testimony in such a grand setting. Still, her testimony disabused the legislators in seconds.

"My name is Juliet Spearwuts. I'm an evolutionary scientist and the founder of The Father's Will Foundation, a lay organization prayerfully dedicated to discerning and protecting God's Holy will. I'm a mother of four strapping boys, and I stand against any proposed legislation that separates God's children from their Creator and conspires to put our Lord out to pasture as if He is outmoded and unable to fulfill his promises to us.

"The arguments I have studied in favor of transhumanism state emphatically that God has reached the end of His usefulness. It concludes that man can no longer sit back and let evolution improve his lot in life, that man has reached the boundaries of God's creativity and the end of natural improvement.

"Further, it declares that man has created and continues to innovate and improve machine learning and the vehicles required to unite mechanical, electronic, and artificial intelligence elements to integrate men's flesh, blood, and brain with the steel, algorithms, and compliance of androids. Thus, they proclaim that this progress is superior because it can be conjured in the minds of men. This notion springs from the same satanic notions that brought us Hitler, Stalin, and Mao. The proponents of Transhumanism share a repudiation and a repugnance of the common man upon which tyrants have built slaughterhouses. They are the experts, the chosen geniuses, the self-proclaimed inheritors of the earth, the humans who would destroy humanity for its own good.

"I implore you to fight this transhumanistic legislation with all you have. The money you would make promoting this legislation is the thirty pieces of silver with which you will hang yourselves. Altering God's plan should not be the work of human hands. If He wants it changed, let Him do it.

"Stand up against this blasphemy. Show some spine. Save your souls. The human race is not your experiment. May God's counsel be in your hearts, and may you hear and follow His Holy will."

The Chairman had better things to do than listen to a witness instead of her party's desires. She'd paid as little attention as possible to Mrs. Spearwuts' statement. In the spare time carved out for the testimony of unessential citizens, she had scheduled a meeting to finalize a secret quid pro quo deal with important foreign agents of an enemy foreign government.

The Chairman's aide was responsible for tapping her on the shoulder so she'd pause her Zoom call when the witnesses completed their opening statements.

When tapped, Democrat Chairman Clampshell's head jerked up as she abruptly interrupted her private meeting and brought her gavel down.

"We thank you for exercising your civic duty. Will the next witness proceed with her preliminary statement? "Please state your name and credentials for the record and give us your opening statement," the Chairman said, ignoring the witness and resuming her Zoom meeting.

"My name is Hilda Wick. I'm from St. Jude's parish in Campwater Meadows, South Dakota. We're a small parish, but our parishioners have big hearts."

Her voice had a squashed sound as if her lips, tongue, and the roof of her mouth were too close together, and her primary means of forming words was her epiglottis. She warbled her "Os" and trilled her "Ls."

Her hayseed credentials and distracting speech were reason enough for most listeners to ignore her words and deny her brilliance. They instinctively tagged her as a lamebrain and missed another bit of genius in a litany of missed academic opportunities.

It was the rare person in this vaunted subcommittee who paid attention to her, let alone took the time to read the transcripts of her testimony later. But Republican Representative Ben Langston was one of that uncommon breed.

The first-term congressman from Hilda Wick's home state had scratched red-ink notes on his written copy of her opening statement. As far as he was concerned, the issue was decided. There was no need to hear the priest. Everyone knew what he had to say even though he hadn't submitted an opening statement. Throughout the past month, he had made his opinions known on countless daytime TV shows. Certain things never changed. Until they did.

"Ms. Wick, I want you to know that the good people of South Dakota are with you here today, a few in body and most in spirit. I am one of them. I'm on your side. There's nothing to be afraid of."

"I can assure you," she interrupted, her voice considerably altered and as distinct as her retort. "I'm not afraid. And I doubt the people of South Dakota are afraid. What I am is angry. Now, I know our duly elected representatives hate angry constituents. I'd advise you to reconsider. I'll jack you up if anyone gets too close to me. I came here to tell my story, and no servant of the people will stop me. I trust that's clear."

"Well, yes. Colorful and very clear. I said I'm on your side, and I meant it."

"Then prove it."

Langston sighed and gulped some water before he started again.

"So, Ms. Wick, do you ride horses?"

"Are you nuts? Of course, I do."

"Well, some folks never have and wouldn't know how it is when a rascally beast gets on up in your face and won't behave. You know how it is?"

"Sure I do, but if you know anything about what you're sayin', you'd have slapped the brute upside the head a bit and then talked real strong, petting him all the time until he calmed down and behaved. You would, wouldn't you?"

"Yes, I would," Langston responded sternly. "So why don't you knock that chip off your shoulder and get a grip on what's going on here? You're the horse with bad manners. Straighten up. And while you're at it, please stop all the gurgling and sputtering. Speak clearly so the city folk can understand you."

The congressmen, awake enough to notice the odd exchange, gasped.

Hilda Wick smiled.

"I like a strong man. You remind me of my late husband, Carl. He didn't stand for no guff. I'm glad you passed my test. What do you want to know?"

"Just tell us what you think about transhumanism and how the need for God has ended."

Ms. Wick's face flushed crimson. She jumped up and slammed both her fists on the witness table. Fr. Finch and Juliet Spearwuts rose, startled by Ms. Wick's eccentric behavior. The Chairman slapped her gavel on anything it found in its way, and she barked her orders at the moon.

"Order! Order! Mr. Langston, get the witness under control! Seargent at Arms! Do something!"

Langston covered his mouth to hide his wide grin. The Seargent at Arms hurried to the witness table and reached out to grab Ms. Wick. But she was spry and settled him down with a quick yank on his wrist, pulling him in front of her on her stretched-out lap, his butt primed for a good spanking. As she raised her free hand to deliver her first swat, Mr. Langston spoke up.

"Hold it, Ms. Wick. That man ain't no boy. You let him go. He was just following orders."

"Yeah," she replied. "There's too much of that going on around here. Get up, you brute!" She swatted him once just to say she had.

"Point taken. Officer, I think Ms. Wick has calmed down. Right, Ms. Wick?"

"No, but I'll behave myself until I'm forced to defend myself again. Someone needs to tell him that I'm paying all y'all's salary."

"That's good enough for me. Now, will you answer my question?"

“I already answered it by my reaction. I won’t stand for any messing with God’s truth. God the Father, God the Son, and God the Holy Spirit, as it was in the beginning, is now and ever shall be, world without end. Amen!”

Langston shifted his attention to Fr. Finch and noted a telltale cringe in his expression. “I have no further questions for Ms. Wick, who I thank for her heartfelt testimony. I yield the remainder of my time.”

He scanned the legislators and gave the chairman a subtle smile. “Whores and killers have more integrity than all of you packed together,” Langston thought as Fr. Finch began his testimony.

CHAPTER EIGHTEEN

When Millie pulled into the driveway, Sarah stood outside her front door with Gabe in her arms. Millie parked and got out, astonished at the size of the boy. He looked like he weighed forty pounds, and just then, Sarah's arm gave way as she let him slide slowly to the landing. Though the boy was big enough to stand, his immature motor functions wouldn't allow it. But he indeed could crawl and navigate obstacles. Backing down the steps, he scrambled to Millie's feet, begging her to pick him up with juvenile sputterings and baby squeals. Millie was enchanted.

Sarah stayed at the front door, a weary look on her face and a slouching posture that surprised Millie, but she was distracted by Gabe's large, cherubic fingers fumbling with her skirt hem. Though tremendous, he was as yet uncoordinated, and the contrast was so humourous that Millie burst into laughter. Sarah wasn't sure if it was joy or ridicule and suddenly ran down the porch stairs and snatched Gabe away from Millie's outstretched arms.

"I'll take him," she said a bit too sharply. "He's getting tired. It's time for his morning nap.

When Millie called Sarah and said she would be heading to Merced in the morning, Sarah was full of joy. But as the day passed and she lay in her bed that night, a knowing doubt began to set roots in her mind, and she fell into a nightmarish sleep that was too sweaty and draining to be benign. Millie had been in her nightmare, and Sarah had difficulty shaking the thought that her friend could be dangerous. She shook her head. "That's absurd," she said under her breath. Millie was her best friend.

Sarah started for the stairs, and Millie opened her trunk and grabbed a small suitcase and a couple of dresses on hangers.

"Is it okay to leave my car parked out here for a while?" she said.

"Sure. It's broad daylight. We can get it into the garage later."

Once inside, Millie was shown to her room. She tossed the suitcase on the bed and hung her clothes in the closet. She went to the bathroom and freshened up.

"Hey," Sarah called. "Don't stay in there forever. Gabe's pouting. He misses you, and he won't sleep."

Millie eventually came to the living room and sat across from Sarah and the boy.

There was an uncomfortable pause before anyone spoke. It was Sarah who spoke first.

"I told you he was big. Didn't I?"

"Yes," Millie replied. "Very big."

Sarah sat quietly for a few seconds. She must have been holding her breath because she started turning red and soon blurted her words in a burst of spray.

"He says he loves you! He says God loves you! I can't take it anymore! He's driving me crazy! Make him stop! Please!"

Millie hurried to her, wrapping her in her arms. "Hang on, Sarah. It's going to be all right. You're not going crazy, and Gabe is not the enemy. You may not believe it now, but I think he is a blessing."

Sarah sobbed. "Of course he is. He's my baby."

"He's more than that. Just look at him all pudgy and pink. He's the happiest baby I've ever seen. Angelic. That's what I'd call him. A cherub."

Sarah wiped her eyes and swiped her face to adjust her expression, but Millie didn't notice a change.

"I think that we need to have that conversation about Simon."

"Now?" Sarah said.

"Now," Millie replied. "You're a tough gal, Sarah. I need you to snap out of this pity party right now. Steven and I need your help, and I can't let you fall apart and leave us hanging. Besides being Gabe's father, Simon Contlerust was a devil. And I killed him."

"What!" Sarah gasped. "You did what?"

"I killed him to save myself and Steven."

"How dare you come here! You killed my boy's father! You bitch! How can you call me 'friend'? Get out of my house right now!"

Millie had been dreading this display for hours. But she was ready for it.

She jumped up and stepped towards Sarah, who was rising herself. Then, with malice of forethought, she delivered a roundhouse slap that knocked Sarah back on her butt and shut her up.

"Now, you're going to sit right there with your mouth shut until I fill you in on all that happened. When I'm done, I'll leave if you tell me to, but I'm willing to bet that you'll be so scared you'll beg me to stay. Now, I love you, but shut up and listen!"

Sarah pouted, but the fire in her eyes flared higher. She wasn't used to being told what to do, especially in her own house. Still, she exhaled and leaned back on the couch, waiting for Millie to explain herself.

"The man you knew as Simon was an imposter, a figment. He had both Steven and me fooled from the beginning. Steven had a fleeting connection with him from when they worked together for the government. He thought it was the same man. I thought he was my father. He wasn't."

Millie paused for a second and took a big breath while keeping her eyes on Sarah. Gabe was at Millie's feet, trying to scramble his large body up on her couch, even though he lacked the musculature and coordination to do it. When Millie began again, her eyes were moist with tears.

"I've tried to avoid even thinking about this, Sarah. It still hurts so much. I didn't want to tell you a thing just to spare you. But when you told me about Gabe speaking to you in your head, I had to come here and tell you all I know."

Sarah's expression had softened a little. Her tensely stretched skin began to relax, and her face opened up as blood once again flowed through her capillaries.

"Go ahead, Millie. I need to know."

So Millie reached back into the memory she'd tried to deny and told the tale of a dedicated patriot who'd come to her just after she'd finished her commitment to the army.

"He was contrite and circumspect as he delicately revealed that I was his daughter. He said he had been a special agent in a secret agency and had burned out after he'd found himself enjoying a particularly savage assassination. He'd been in rehab for two years. I figured he'd been in the brig.

"He was patient with me, and I believed his story in time. After all, he knew every detail of my mom's family. She was his sister.

"Time passed, and we got closer. Then one day, he came to me and asked me to take a ride with him. He wanted to introduce me to some of his friends. He drove me to a shack on the outskirts of town. That's where you and I first met. That's where we made plans to raid Steven's house and steal the serum. But you know all that."

Sarah was becoming anxious, trying to be patient. Then Millie finally came to the part Sarah knew nothing about.

"It turns out that Simon was using all of us. After Steven rounded us up, Simon snuck into the jail and killed everyone. Except, of course, you and me. You'd been kidnapped and weren't there. Not knowing what had happened, I returned to Steven's house with Simon. Then we joined forces.

Sarah was getting impatient. "Just tell me why you killed him!"

Millie took a big breath and reached out for Gabe, pulling him up so he could sit next to her.

Sarah heard him speaking to her. "What she tells you is the truth though she doesn't know how deep it goes."

Sarah's eyes bulged, and Millie, seeing it as a sign to get to the point, blurted it out all at once.

"He was Satan's pawn. He had powers none of us saw before our final battle. He could change his appearance, construct hallucinations at will, and rejuvenate at will. He was a demon. He was killing Steven, and I had to do something. I shot him several times, and all he did was smile and mock Christ Crucified. Then he repaired his body, and the earth opened up beneath him. He dropped into the chasm with a lurid smile on his face. The pit closed. It was over."

Sarah's mouth was agape. Gabe looked at Millie and gestured to be put back on the floor. He crawled to his mother, and she pulled him into her arms.

Then he spoke his first real words to her. "It's alright, Mommy."

Sarah burst into tears.

"We know who wins in the end," he said, putting his hand on her heart.

CHAPTER NINETEEN

I am Fr. Ezekiel Finch, special emissary to the United Nations serving as ethicist to the Science of Accelerated Evolution Committee."

He spoke without a transcript because he didn't need reminders.

"I possess PhDs in Artificial Intelligence, Evolutionary Biology, and Theological Ethics. It is my pleasure to appear before you today to dispel the hysterical assumptions of the previous witnesses."

A glance at his inquisitors confirmed that most of them were busy on their phones diddling with something far removed from the weighty issues of the day.

"I welcome your questions and intend to support the legislation at hand with science and theology. Instead of denying mankind the opportunity to accelerate God's evolutionary plan, I will promote His creature's brilliant discoveries and put an end to the heresies promoted by my fellow witnesses."

The Chairman's eyes opened a little wider, and a smile spread across her face. She had just acted on a tip by shifting One Hundred Thousand dollars of campaign donations into stock options in a fledgling company whose diverse products included cryogenic life extension. This company also held patents on wireheading, no longer a sci-fi fantasy, where physical connections are implanted in brains to induce pleasurable responses for doing their controller's bidding. The priest's statement sent thrills down her spine.

Even as she prepared to begin the questioning of witnesses, her stock-market app flashed a three-fold increase in her investment. She could redeem her campaign funds and get them redeposited before anyone knew they were missing.

"We will begin our first round of questioning," she said. "Ms. Uwibajije, you have five minutes."

Outlier Democrat Representative Lilly Uwibajije was a beauty, self-possessed, poised, and confident. Her raven hair was silky, her skin as smooth as her Nigerian ancestor's. She was a native of a village of martyred souls, and her name meant "follow God's plan." Every dog, man, woman, and child had been raped and decapitated except for Lilly and her father. They had lain in a pile of pig shit, terrified, their noses and eyes exposed, staring without blinking at the genocide unfolding before them. They had survived, eventually landing on America's shores, kissing the earth of Freedom's home, and making it their own. As a citizen, she carried herself regally, for she was following God's plan with an ax to grind.

"I will address my first question to each of you in turn," she said, peering over half-readers. "When did God die? You first, Mrs. Spearwuts. When did God die?"

Juliet Spearwuts was caught mid-stream with a mouthful of water heading past her vocal cords. She choked when she heard the question and nearly spat her water back into her glass, garbling her words. With hysterical gestures, she proclaimed for the world and heavens, "God is not dead!"

"And you, Ms. Wick. Can you be more demonstrative than Ms. Spearwuts?"

Hilda Wick stared daggers at the committee, her eyes roaming from one to the next, hesitating on each legislator's face until they raised their eyes from the daddling and surfing that occupied most of their time as servants of the people.

Her effort started slowly but increased more rapidly as those yet to be confronted looked up to see why the room had gone silent.

With continually accelerating success, Ms. Wick caught the eye of each one of the people's representatives. Satisfied, she returned her sharp gaze to Representative Uwibajije.

"God is eternal and, by definition, cannot die," Ms. Wick stated undeniably.

"Exactly," the junior statesman replied. "And accepting that truth is a foundational principle of your belief, is it not?"

"Yes," the two women said in unison.

Father Finch was unmoved.

"Are you a member of a particular faith, Ms. Wick? Ms. Spearwuts?"

"I'm a Roman Catholic," Ms. Wicks replied, her jaw lifted in defiance.

"As am I," Ms. Spearwuts concurred.

"That brings us to you, Fr. Finch. What is your answer? Is God dead?"

The sardonic twist in Fr. Finch's smile was subtle, yet Representative Uwibajije caught its malevolence, having seen such smiles on the savages of her youth.

"Perhaps," he said quietly. "Who's to say?"

Representative Uwibajije's answer was swift and meant to sting.

"Who's to believe, Fr. Finch?"

With that, the chairman came alive. "The Representative's time has expired. The Chair recognizes the Republican Representative from Texas, John Skelton."

Skelton was a sun-wrinkled, leather-faced rancher who chose his words carefully and suckered many a witness into thinking he was a hayseed putz.

"Tell me, Fr. Finch. Who is your Bishop?"

"The Bishop of Rome."

"Is that the Pope?"

"Do you have another in mind?"

"Please answer the question. Are you referring to the Pope?"

"This is ridiculous and has nothing to do with my testimony."

"You're mistaken, Fr. Finch. Is your relationship with the Pope ecclesiastical or presumptive?"

"Do you mean to insult me?"

"I mean to get a straight answer from you. Is the Pope your Bishop?"

"You're calling me a liar?"

"No, I'm calling you the Master of Lies."

Fr. Finch burst out laughing. "Satan? Don't be foolish."

"If not Satan, then his top student. You were deceitful when you were so kind as to let the ladies go first. That wasn't chivalry. It was deception."

"I object to the congressman's insults," the representative from New York said.

The chairman nodded. "Mr. Skelton will keep a civil tongue."

"Very well," Skelton said. "Here's what I know. There is no record of you having been vested. If you did take vows, I expect they were to a force set against the love of God. You are undoubtedly a religious zealot, but you are not a Catholic Priest.

"You are a charlatan whose goal and religion is to be God; to create a privileged class who will play God, born to subjugate the unwashed by belittling their fear of God, their love of God, and transfering their public authority to unworthy morons incapable of reason and wisdom. Convinced that freedom would be theirs if they complied, they would become a slave class crushed by fear.

"Your written testimony shows us that, and your claim of academic accomplishment cannot be found.

"You are kin to Satan. Perhaps His minion. You have perjured yourself, and I call for this committee to hold you in contempt of Congress."

The cries from the other side of the aisle rose in a single roar like a choir of rats *In the First Circle*.

"My time is up," Representative Skelton said and leaned back in his chair, his ruddy complexion capturing the best light for the camera.

New York Democrat Representative Constance Grundle's attention lingered on the Texas Representative for two beats longer than necessary, and she lost the sharp edge of her entrance in vainglory. Her moment lost, she soldiered on.

"Ad hominem attacks are your specialty, aren't they, Mr. Skelton?"

Skelton replied out of turn. "Stop with the Latin. You don't know what it means."

CHAPTER TWENTY

Gabe Contlerust sat up in his crib in the dead of night, his eyes wide open, his ears perked for the slightest sound. A whisp of a southerly breeze rippled the sheer curtains, and the scent of an approaching storm filled his nose with moist, earthly scents. His little smile widened with joy. Life's cycle was intact, and all the absurdity of humankind, the unappreciated gifts that God had given to his creation, all the denial, arrogance, and blasphemy that the coming day would face could not diminish the boy's love of life so dear. His smile remained even as he sorted the unnumbered transgressions of the day to come. Wisdom and truth graced the child with an ancient mind. The Wisdom of God was his inheritance and his calling. He was the messenger of God sent to carry out his Father's will.

Notwithstanding the boy's intellect, his body coordination developed at a human rate. At 2:00 AM, he let out a sob heard throughout the house, and his mother was at his side in a moment. Millie got out of bed as well and headed to the kitchen to warm up the coffee. When Sarah joined her, Gabe was already murmuring and softly nursing, his eyes closed in sleep.

The two friends sat quietly for a few minutes. Millie then poured herself a cup of coffee and a glass of water for Sarah. It was a peaceful moment, quiet, soothing.

A startling crack of lightning lit the room with cold light, and seconds later, the thunderclap rattled the house, and Gabe's eyes snapped open. He let out a wail that pierced the night, and suddenly all was still. The electric storm didn't materialize, and the thunder passed in silence.

The expected rain moved on down the line. All the Earth was at peace again, and Gabe smiled.

A few minutes later, he touched his mother's cheek and spoke to her mind.

"Millie's husband is in great danger. We need to warn him. I've told him to call her right now."

Sarah was beginning to accept his telepathy, yet it remained a stunning surprise when she heard his voice, mature and educated, in her head. It took her a beat to react.

"Mom," Gabe said. "Let Millie know. Okay?"

Before Sarah could open her mouth, the phone rang. It was 3:33 AM. Gabe gurgled bubbles and hummed with pleasure at the moment.

"Grab the phone, will you, Millie? It's for you."

Millie raised her eyebrows but caught on right away.

"Hello? Steven? Hello, darling. I miss you."

Her smile faded, and a full minute passed before she muttered, "Yes. I understand. But I need to be with you."

Another long pause, and she looked at Sarah for support but only saw bewilderment that matched hers in return.

"Tell him to come here," Sarah said, grasping at straws.

Millie shook her head. "I understand. I don't like it, though. I know, but there must be something I can do to help."

Popoford spoke again; this time, his voice was strong enough for Sarah to hear.

"I can't risk you getting hurt. You must stay with Sarah. Don't let her or the child out of your sight. Especially the child. I have to get whatever is messing with my head straightened out, and I want you as far away from the danger as possible. I love you, and you love me. Pray for all of us that we can survive the hell that has infected the world."

"You sound crazy, Steven."

He didn't answer her, but she heard his voice clearly in her head.

"I am crazy. Crazy for you. Crazy for life. Now promise me you will pray for me."

She replied without speaking. "Always, love."

Popoford quietly ended the call but not before he made a request of Gabe. He asked him to convince his mother to leave Merced. Take Millie with her and disappear. They all were in danger and needed to hide.

Gabe's message back to Popoford was simple and confident. "Be not afraid. You have guardians round about you. Ask for their help when you need it. You have been chosen. Do your part well."

CHAPTER TWENTY-ONE

When Representative Skelton accused Representative Constance Grundle of being too ignorant of Latin to use common phrases to rebuke him, there was a moment of silence as before the executioner's ax dropped on the convicted's neck.

Saving the day, the Chairman's gavel thwacked her sounding block so powerfully that the gavel's head flew forward and slammed into the back of Democrat Representative Stub, who had been softly snoring since the hearing began. He jumped up from his seat, screaming, "Murder! Murder!" Five full minutes passed before Representative Grundle could speak. "Madam Chairman. I insist that order be kept in this chamber. Respect for constituents, witnesses, and fellow Assembly Members must be enforced."

There was a general snicker throughout the room. With chagrin, Representative Grundle reclaimed her time and proceeded to question the witnesses.

"Now, ladies, I will take my time to ask you what you know about your understanding of God's will for mankind. Obviously, your faith is strong. Doubtless, you are unmovable in your beliefs. It is not my purpose to change your minds, but I want to see if you understand the nuances of the business before us today. Now. Ms. Spearwuts. Juliet, correct?"

"Yes."

"Fine. Can you explain how the ability of man to create once-unforeseen technology and use their God-given intellect to advance science for the betterment of mankind can be 'blasphemous and the work of the Devil?' Those are your words in your written testimony. Will you expand on what you wrote?"

"We know that many things are within man's reach that he should avoid for the sake of his immortal soul. Just because it can be done doesn't mean it is acceptable to God. Quite the contrary. We have the Ten Commandments as our guide. It is the law that God gave us, the first informing all others: "I am the LORD your God: you shall not have strange Gods before me." We believe God is immutable, beyond the confines of time or space. He is wisdom itself, and He can't be supplanted by anyone or anything."

"Well," Grundle said, mimicking Jack Benny. "That doesn't leave much room for open minds."

"The truth is available to everyone, even those whose closed minds reject it."

"Ms. Spearwuts, your dogmatic position will get us nowhere."

"I pray that's the case."

Representative Grundle rolled her eyes as if flipping off a child as she raised her hands to the heavens for intercession; the same heavens she was sure were a figment of mass hysteria. Titters rolled through the room from both sides of the aisle, even from representatives who campaigned on their devout faith.

"And you, Ms. Wick, do you have a nuanced, more collegial opinion?"

"I don't use words like collegial when speaking to a bitch," she said, her eyes glued to Grundle's. And the room erupted.

Shouts of "Decorum!" echoed off the walls. Legislators rose en masse to silence the witness, Constitutional rights notwithstanding.

Hilda Wick drove the spike through their hearts when the House was finally gaveled to silence.

"In the real world, a bitch is a girl dog. Representative Grundle is a dog!"

With that, she rose, straightened her skirt, and asked Juliet Spearwuts to join her. Together, heads held high, they left the People's House and walked out into the real world, already revered as patriotic heroes.

Outrage and dead silence lasted only a minute, broken and forgotten, when the Chairman addressed Representative Trent, "You have five minutes."

CHAPTER TWENTY-TWO

Steven Popoford, once a confused and deceived assassin for the corrupted federal agency known as Home Office, had lived a short life of sanity. Only those months after Contlerust was crushed could be counted as sane. Only the days he was discerning baptism and his celibate time with Millie could be considered real life. That and the day they were married, plus the morning after. Everything before and after was a scramble of lies, deceit, and Hell. So here it was again. The terror and frustration. The confusion. The lack of normalcy, whatever that was.

He sat alone in the woods just beyond the treeline. He had been there for two hours after he hung up the phone. Still, motionless as the dead of night. He was quiet as an owl swooping through the moonlit glimmer, eyes latched on the prize, unnoticed even at the last second when death sliced through the night and snatched its prey. His breath condensed into a fog the cool air. Something odd was happening, and the day was sure to be unseasonably hot.

Popoford looked over his shoulder into the black woods. He'd heard a sound, soft, so light, almost tender, more delicate than the near-silent touch of a wolf's paw on the sand. And there it was again, closer.

He stood slowly, simultaneously shifting his pistol to his right hand and picking up the semi-auto shotgun lying on his lap. The pistol slipped smoothly into his belt holster, his right hand rising to the shotgun's forend. As smoothly as he had risen, he squatted behind the stump he'd been on and held his breath.

All of Popoford's senses locked onto the approaching sound. He let his breath out with care and inhaled again without creating any sound. His every synapse was cocked and ready to fire. His nerves were stinging, crying for action. But the next step never came, and Popoford got tired of the night watch, and a drowsy fog muddled his mind.

"There's no place like home, Dorothy once said."

Popoford lept into the air.

"I think it's time to bring you home, Steven. Home to the new Home Office. The GNU."

Popoford's feet hit the ground in a combat stance; knees bent, feet offset, body leaning forward, his shotgun raised to his eye, his finger bringing up the trigger slack.

"Pull the trigger, Steven, if it makes you happy. It will not harm anything except your soul. But what can that matter? What you have done in your lifetime qualifies you for a black eternity with my Master."

Popoford emptied the shotgun's magazine. The dwarf's head blew into chunks of flesh and bone, pools of blood and mucus in every direction. Popoford was splashed with the liquid, and his hands and face were sliced with the dwarf's fragmented skull. He slumped onto one knee, wiping the mess from his face, fluttering his eyelids to clear his vision.

The creature that dragged him from his house lay dead at his feet. The monster that had injected him with some potion that caused him to read minds and to leave his brain subject to suggestion and downright hypnotic control was dead.

Popoford would have stomped the man if the corpse still had a head. Instead, he kicked the lifeless body in the gut as hard as possible.

"That feels good, doesn't it, Steven?"

Popoford froze with his foot about to launch a second vengeful strike.

"Do what you will, Steven. You are in my power, and nothing can harm me, especially you."

Popoford raised his hands and turned slowly in the direction of the voice, the same direction as the sound of muffled paws.

"Who was that?" Popoford said.

"The headless one is someone you know, one of my menagerie."

"An animal?"

"If you like. Do you like to torture animals, Steven?"

Popoford was silent.

"Oh, did I hurt your feelings? Good. It's time for you to bow to your master. Can you bow that low, Steven?"

Popoford felt his muscles contract and his body folded tightly, beyond all possibilities, into an eight-inch crumple, his eyes peeking out above his feet, his ears smashed between his knees, and his chin buried in the forest floor.

Contlerust rose out of the dwarf's form and strode to the stump that Popoford had used. He sat on it, raised his legs, then lowered them onto Popoford's squashed body as if on a hassock.

"It's Steven, the forest ottoman," Contlerust snickered. "All the comforts of home wherever I go. Jealous, Steven? Don't be. You could take my place any time you want. The boss is looking for a few good men. No pun intended."

Contlerust crossed his legs and produced a riding crop. He tapped Popoford's nose with twelve bars of a Louie Bellson riff.

"You like the music, Steven? It kind of gets you jumpin', doesn't it? Let's see your moves."

With that, the crop was applied with vigor to Popoford's butt as Contlerust dramatically commanded, "Dance, boy, dance!" And he whistled a happy tune.

"If ever you feel afraid, hold your head erect!" he ordered.

Popoford's body unfolded in a snap!

"And whistle a happy tune!"

Popoford puckered his lips and did as he was ordered, but only a dry, inharmonious whoosh escaped his mouth.

"And no one will know you're afraid!"

Popoford was terrified.

"Dance, clown, dance!" Contlerust bellowed, and the woods echoed his devilish spew.

Suddenly he yelled a curse loud enough to startle the entire world and jammed the crop between Popoford's legs causing him to tumble headlong onto the forest floor.

"What a clutz," Contlerust laughed. "What a putz."

Popoford raged within as he slowly rose to his knees and then to his feet. Looking around, he saw Contlerust with his back cranked toward the heavens, his mouth agape as if his scream was still reverberating. There was no sign of the headless dwarf. Had there ever been a dwarf? Contlerust was there. Or was he?

Popoford shook his head, hoping clarity would return, and when he opened his eyes again, the sun had risen, and Contlerust was gone.

But it wasn't that nothing had happened. His shotgun was lying on the ground. He picked it up and checked the magazine. Only one shell had been fired. The husk was on the ground. Popoford had pulled the trigger, and that meant that something had happened. But what? Having only recently experienced the earth rolling beneath his feet, he couldn't be sure that anything he thought was real. Only a few things were certain: The dwarf had injected something into his carotid artery, he could read certain minds, and Contlerust was back.

As he stood there exhausted and wondering what to do, he heard the unmistakable voice of a boy.

He did what Gabe told him to do and returned to the cabin to call Millie at Sarah's house.

When he hung up the phone, he rested his head on the kitchen table and slid into a petrifying dream.

CHAPTER TWENTY-THREE

Representative Buck Trent whispered to his assistant, then turned back to his microphone. With a smile he practiced in the mirror each morning, the Republican was the most photogenic public servant on Capital Hill. His handsome, youthful exterior seemed never to age, and some placed private bets on the location of his corrupted "Dorian Gray" picture. Publically he was loved by all as he enjoyed increasing wealth while taking his daily orders from the masters of the technosphere. Privately, he was despised as a sham, a dolt, and a slimebag. He couldn't have cared less since his re-election was guaranteed for as long as he voted as Contlerust told him to in whispers to his soul. Trent was a kept man.

"Fr. Finch, Welcome. I have read your testimony and am intrigued by the depth of your knowledge of evolution and the fact that humans have stalled in their march to perfection. As a man of God, will you enlighten my colleagues? I understand that whether God is dead or alive has nothing to do with your support of this important legislation. Is that true?"

Contlerust spoke silently to his Master and thanked him for providing this pompous simpleton. He then returned to his pastoral character and spoke out loud.

"Thank you, Congressman. I am pleased to have a logical conversation with you and others. The heated irrationality of emotion, usually called faith, gets in the way of man's limited acuity and stifles mental progress."

"And how do you define mental progress, Father," Trent asked, harkening to his High School debating class where the demand that an opponent define his terms became the end-all in debate success.

"I define it by the degree of acceptance one finds in the substance of arguments put forth by men of science and by the willingness a person has in discarding presumptive notions that have ruled their lives for the enlightened truths established by thought leaders of the modern world. None of us can know everything, and most of us don't waste time pursuing subjects we can never understand. It's best to have an abiding faith in those who are experts than to indulge a gut feeling or sentiment that is at odds with scientific truth."

"Your explanation is most welcome, Father," Trent said. "Tell me, what do you say to the laypeople of your congregation when they cite apologists of old like Thomas Aquinas or C. K. Chesterson?"

"'The old order changeth yielding place to new, And God fulfills himself in many ways, Lest one good custom should corrupt the world to the new.' Is it not true that we have accepted many changes in our lives as we grow, even as mankind has accepted change overcoming rebellion and sycophancy always to remain true believers of God's will?"

"I suppose you're right," was Trent's dull answer. He had no idea what Finch meant. "So, do you have any advice for the faithful who are hesitant in embracing the genius and inevitability of using our God-given gifts to design electronics and machines to evolve at a pace that God Himself allows? Is this not God's design to increase our intelligence beyond our human nature so we can embrace the eternal peace He has promised?"

"You express my position perfectly."

Those who knew Buck Trent also knew that the questions he asked were not of his making. He was too dull to understand the words he spoke, too dense to grasp the most straightforward consequences of their meaning. Having no thoughts of his own, he bowed out.

"Thank you, Fr. Finch. You have brought clarity to the Church and true believers everywhere. After your testimony, anyone who objects to this legislation should be considered an enemy of the human race. Canceling and imprisonment may not be sufficient punishments for these traitors to mankind's future. Disappearing them may be the only way to cleanse the world's population for the good of all 'suitable' mankind."

"I appreciate your words, Mr. Trent, but I hesitate to encourage direct action against those who oppose the inevitable. Let society, in its finesse, deal with them. Those without approved levels of intelligence will have their place in society. The working class needs reinforcements, and scrupulous souls have always populated the workhouses and chain gangs, have they not?"

"Undoubtedly," Trent said. "I relinquish my remaining time."

The Representatives were in pleased turmoil as Chairman Clampshell gavelled the session to a vote. It was lunchtime, and the lead witness had delivered the administration's message. After the necessary parliamentary procedures, the question was put to the vote and passed nineteen to three.

The legislative day had ended, and lunchtime and meetings with lobbyists would fill their afternoons. Dinner, drinks, and cigars would follow with side events where deals pure and nefarious would be signed and sealed, all for the betterment of the people's representatives, their constituencies be damned.

Contlerust left the chamber to the rhythm of flashing strobes and disappeared into the first shadowed corridor he could find. When he returned to the light, he was a tragic figure ripe for ignoring or scorn. Only the powerful were noteworthy. Only the cream of the intelligentsia is memorable. Mankind outside the center of power did not influence international policy. No one cared about the life of a dwarf, an evident argument against God's goodness, and those who saw him leave the Capital Building forgot him at once.

CHAPTER TWENTY-FOUR

Between the time Popoford heard the boy's voice in his head and he picked up the phone to call Millie, a script ran through his mind, a part in which he was a tragic hero playing alongside Millie's fateful love.

It was the final scene, and an obsidian sword was thrust into his gut. Slow, painful death was upon him. His blood flowed down the sword's shaft. Damned by his hands clutching the sword's razor edge, his blood was diverted and flowed down his arms. The drip sped up and became a river on the dirt and dust beneath his feet. Too thick to seep into the soil, it eventually pooled into an impossible pond. In its tangy sweetness, the flies came to suck; the lizards came to snatch the fattened flies, then the rats, dogs, wolves, and buzzards played their parts. Hyenas, in turn, traced a circle of death back to Popoford, falling to his knees, his eyes locked on the yellow eyes of Contlerust, whose appetite was personified in the drool flowing from his mouth into the same pool where Popoford's blood had spilled. And the mad canines locked their jaws onto his legs, pulling him to the ground and through the pool of his blood.

And he heard another voice in his head, saccharine, insinuating, and insulting.

"What a sweet boy you are, Steven. So sweet yet so dull. I have shown you my power. I have invited you to follow me. Yet you mock me with your fear. There is no fear attached to me. The power I offer is without hooks. You owe me nothing and never will. As far as I'm concerned, you can just go to Hell!"

Contlerust burst into a thunderous, spastic laugh bending double and thumping his head as if celebrating a triumphant victory.

"Don't you see, Steven? Go to Hell? Don't you get it?"

Popoford's mental exhaustion didn't keep him from exploding in a rage. He tried to expel the whispering Screwtape by slamming his fists against his temples. All that did was give him a grievous headache. He then shook his head too hard, and the headache got worse. He fell to his knees and let out a silent wide-mouthed scream of Munch insanity. Then something snapped inside him.

A sharp pop, then a dull pain radiated through Popoford's brain. He let his head sink to the floor and relished the cool relief. His breathing steadied and slowed. He sighed and raised his head high enough to wipe his brow. Blinking his one eye until it cleared, he stood up on wobbly legs.

He looked around to be sure he was alone. Then, the boy's voice gently called his name.

"Steven, the time has come. The demon's virus in you has been split in two. The space where we are talking right now is hidden from him. Come here when you want to speak freely. The other place is public, and he hears everything. But you are not safe. No one is safe. A hundred thousand souls are still afflicted with the same worm you have, with thousands more infected daily. Millions upon millions more are under Satan's whispering influence. Even more are bound to Him by a damning blood oath. You know too much to ignore the path shown to you. Pick up your sword and shield and follow the path before you.

There is no other way but the path of righteousness for you."

Popoford was stunned. Deep in his heart, he knew how to respond, but a voice masquerading as wisdom told him to go slowly. Still, the child would have none of it.

"Snap out of it, Steven. You know what must be done. You have been called. Accept His call with modesty and grace. Now!"

Popoford instinctively crossed himself and turned to gaze at the picture of the Blessed Virgin Mary that hung on his wall. With a deep breath, he girded himself and answered, "Yes."

"Well done, Steven. Now pick up your phone and call Sarah's house. Millie will answer."

"What will I say?"

"I'll help you with the conversation."

He nodded his head just as Millie answered the phone.

"Hello? Steven? Hello, darling. I miss you."

With her words of love, his resolve was sealed.

CHAPTER TWENTY-FIVE

When Popoford hung up the phone, he stood quite still. He was in the room where he had first met Millie, in the house where they were to make their home. Their plans, sketchy as they were, contained all he wished for. But the idyllic married life naturally expected by newlyweds had shredded into a pernicious stew. If bliss were ever to be theirs, it would be postponed.

The boy's voice, inserted in his thought, was gentle yet specific.

"There is a plan, Steven, that you must understand and follow as closely as possible. It's not going to be easy. What great good has ever come easily? It will be the hardest thing you have ever done. Yet with faith, your hardships can prove beneficial."

"What must I do?" Popoford asked.

"You must follow through with this Dark Angel and become his servant."

Popoford was stunned. "You're the Devil's spawn! Get behind me, Satan!"

"No, Steven, I may be shrewd, but I'm certainly not what you say I am. What I am is the messenger of God. You know my name."

"It's Gabe, right?"

"I am the Archangel Gabriel, Messenger of God. He has sent me to tell you that you will embrace the demon known as Contlerust, serve him as he wishes, and make yourself his confidant. All this you will do because you wish to please your God. His ways are beyond your understanding, but you will lead the demon down the path of destruction."

"And how can I do that with Contlerust watching my every move?'

"The Holy Spirit will be with you in times of trouble and joy. Listen to your heart for the Holy Spirit's wisdom. Listen to your mind for my direction."

Popoford, wishing he had never answered the door to the dwarf, now forced himself to stay calm. He was not the most humble person in the world. Indeed, he felt he had been anointed by what was being asked of him. And he wasn't the most righteous person ever born, yet he surprised himself with what came out of his mouth.

"I am the Lord's servant. Let it be done to me as you have said."

A warmth washed over Popoford that he had never known. "Jesus," he said, "You take care of it."

With that, the conversation with Gabe was over, and Popoford was alone. He sat at the kitchen table and put his head down on his crossed arms. There he stayed until the sun had ducked behind the treetops. It was three thirty-three. Then the minute hand moved, and he heard Contlerust's gentle voice grazing his thoughts like a lover's lips on expectant flesh. Popoford fought an urge to clench every muscle and forced himself to remain placid, waiting for the seducer to sink his teeth into his soul.

"Oh, my sweet morsel. What's to become of you? Have you been a good boy since I was gone? Let me guess. No. Right?"

Popoford conquered his impulses, exhaled, relaxed, and answered as calmly as he could.

"I have been waiting for you. I've been waiting for your orders."

Popoford couldn't tell if time had slowed or had hurried up. It seemed like hours had passed, yet when Contlerust answered, it was only a beat. His heart sank with the knowledge that he had committed to join the demon's corp. Still, his faith rose again when he heard the gentle sound of Gabe, the toddler, breathing, steadfast and true.

"I can't believe what I'm hearing," Contlerust smirked. "Little Stevie Popoford makes a grownup decision. What do you say to that?"

A triumphal roar rose, which might have bellowed from the Black Angel himself. The earth's bowels gurgled and belched sulfuric renewables and flung his venom through every earthly fissure, be they volcanoes, geysers, crevasses, or the mouths of enslaved humans. All Hell was busting buttons in prideful displays. The dark realm had secured the soul Satan's right-hand man had sought for many years. And this one showed promise to lead the legions of Hell against St. Michael the Archangel and crush all the souls and angels of Heaven. All black-hearted spirits joined in one curdling voice celebrating the impending fall of God.

In Sarah's spare bedroom, Millie covered her head with a pillow and wept. She didn't notice Sarah entering the room until her friend sat on the bed. Millie caught her breath and hoped she had hidden her despair. But it was too late.

"You haven't picked this road of suffering, Millie, but you must steel yourself for what is to come."

"What do you mean?"

"I know about Steven's call and what has been asked of him."

Millie lay stunned for half a minute before dragging the pillow from her head. She let it fall to the floor and searched for Sarah's eyes. Finding a glint reflected from the hall light and an unconscious batting of eyes, she gazed at Sarah's silhouette and rose to sit on the edge of the bed.

"What do you know? Tell me everything. All of it, Sarah. What's happening?"

"Your husband's been sent on a mission, you know, sent by God."

Millie wagged her head but what Sarah had said stayed in her memory. "This is a dream, right? I'm not here. You're not here. It's just something I ate and a dose of dope. Right? That's right, isn't it?

The reflection in Sarah's eyes wagged in answer. "You know what I'm saying is true. Steven must have told you."

"All he said was that he loved me."

Sarah was silent again.

"What is it? Tell me! What do you know?"

But Sarah didn't answer. She didn't have to because Gabe had crawled into the room, and with a grace far beyond his age, he rose from his knees and stood upright, steady on his feet, his face aglow with an inner light. Sarah grasped Millie and wrapped her arms around her to quiet her own astonishment and pacify Millie's. Together, they cowered in fear.

"My Lord has said, 'Be not afraid. I go before you. Come follow me.' Heed what He has said and be at peace. I bring you glad tidings from on high."

With that, Gabe fell silent and cocked his head slightly as if listening to the cooing of a dove deep in the forest at daybreak. In the darkened room, two hearts beating rapidly slowed to a measured calm. Neither Millie nor Sarah felt any anxiety. Serenity filled their souls, and the words of the Blessed Mother came to them both. "Let it be done to me according to your word."

The explanation Millie once wanted, and Sarah couldn't truly deliver, was no longer needed. This blessing soothed their souls almost completely, for Sarah was at rest. But Millie harbored a desire to act, to find Steven and be by his side. To be his wife, a helpmate in times of trouble. It gnawed at her, and she averted her eyes from Gabe.

And he knew what she wanted and spoke to her in a voice Sarah could not hear.

"You must go to him, Millie. But not without the armor of the Lord. Accept His will over you and stand with Steven. He has not turned his back on God but is following the path he has been shown. Give him strength and love, and your way will also be fulfilled.

"Where can I find him?"

"In a place of Hell's own making," Gabe said to her telepathically. "In a meeting of demons and sycophants, spirits and flesh, plotting the confusion and conflagration of the entire earth. Go to him, for together you are the human tools that may yet aid St. Michael to cast into Hell Satan and all the demons who prowl about the world seeking the ruin of souls. Go, and play your part well."

As Millie slowly returned from her telepathic communication with Gabe, she was alone in the bedroom. Startled at missing Sarah and Gabe leaving the room, she was even more surprised to find herself alone in the house.

"Hey! Where are you?" she cried, but there was no answer. She looked everywhere in the house and opened the door to the setting sun as it provided its last measure of light before dusk. She had been standing in the bedroom unconscious for hours and had no idea where Sarah had gotten to.

She called her home in Whimsy in desperation, hoping Steven was there. Finally, she hung up and had to reflect on Gabe's words to get her feet on the ground and figure out what she had to do to find her husband.

Millie was frantic and rushed out of the house without closing the front door. She paced back and forth about the clearing when Steven's soothing voice suddenly filled her head.

"I can't talk long. I have a caretaker who keeps a close eye on me. Just know that I love you, and everything will be okay."

"That's not true, Steven. You have a job, and so have I. Please tell me where you are and how I can get there. I've got a job to do myself, and I mean to get it done. We're working for the same boss. We're working together. Boss's orders."

She could almost hear Popoford smile.

"Got to go," he said. "I'll send you directions when I know where I am."

"Stay safe, darling," Millie said. "Help is on the way."

CHAPTER TWENTY-SIX

Contlerust's body shifted into Arthur Harcourt. He slid his passkey over the lock scanner, and the double doors swung open to GNU's circular meeting room. Then, with his arm wrapped around Popoford's shoulder, he dramatically presented his prize like he would a manikin clothed in sartorial splendor. Everyone looked up in amazement, for they instantly realized they were witnessing the anointing of the chosen one, the man who stood at the right hand of their spiritual leader.

Harcourt's glare stifled the gathering's groans of dismay, and each impending frown uplifted into a smile. Yet none of them could hide their rage, contempt, and disappointment from Harcourt. He glared into their eyes as he advanced into the room with Popoford, a privileged family member, a made man, heir to the throne.

When he finally reached his chair, Harcourt offered Popoford a seat next to him.

Harcourt, who was, in fact, Satan's right hand, Asmodai, the second most devious spirit since the Creation, now sat on the throne alongside his disciple. Whether presenting himself for who he was or disguising himself in myriad flesh and blood costumes, there was no more significant threat to the wandering human mind than this betrayer of God's blessing save for Satan himself.

Before him, he saw not compatriots in an ancient war but goats and patsies, all lacking a trait dear to tyrants and saviors alike, that of humility, for one to contain the spirit and for the other to set it free.

He finally raised his hand, signaling his sycophant polyglot to sit and shut up. It was his floor. His meeting. His time to rule.

Yet in his tone, he gave up nothing of his intrigue, his malevolent vision that saw them all burning in Hell surrounding the eternal pyre of the fallen Black Angel with flames tended by St. Michael. His arrogance was pure egotism, the most refined of the deadly sins. He not only compared himself to Satan but also embraced the greatest heresy. He compared himself to God the Father.

"You are stunned, my dear friends. All your hopes have melted away. There is no future for you. You think I have picked a stooge to lead us to victory. You think I have lost my mind. You think you will mount a righteous rebellion, and Satan will join you in it. I advise you to correct your malfunctioning heads. There is no hope, but you forgot that. Neither is there rebellion; you forgot that as well.

"Now," Harcourt ordered. "Stand and be counted. Salute your earthly leader. Pledge yourselves to his success by your eternal suffering. Rise, my loyal horde! Fail me now, and you will know Hell's fury here, now, and forever.

"I said, 'now!' Jump up! Pledge yourselves or burn!"

As one, they responded, not in an instantaneous leap of faith but with a universal hesitancy. First, by setting pencils just so on blank tablets and adjusting their chairs. Then, straightening their ties and skirts, they stood without enthusiasm, and three decided not to salute Popoford. Harcourt had no choice but to pass his sentence and execute his threatened verdict. To dither was to lose.

Harcourt didn't reach for a wand, nor did he gather the forces of evil unto himself and smite the recalcitrant lot of them. Instead, he put a thought in Popoford's head, and the execution proceeded without fuss.

"Read my mind, Steven. The three standing behind the others plan to destroy me and claim you for themselves. Melt their brains, Steven. Just will it, and it will be so."

Popoford lived a dual existence as a free human and a demon's slave. First, he nurtured thoughts to make Contlerust think he was totally under his control. Then, he shifted his true thoughts into Gabe's protected channel so he could go undiscovered as he planned Contlerust's death.

He straightened up when the order came to eliminate the condemned GNU traitors. Then, with silent but deadly thought, he gathered the power of all the delegate's minds while generating an electrical current strong enough to fry the synapses of the disloyal three. They collapsed as one, flopping on the floor like panicked fish until they evaporated. Their demon cohorts acted as if nothing had happened.

The roar that Harcourt raised in the stillness rattled the rafters. As it dissipated, the silence was overwhelming, and Popoford slumped in his chair. But the remaining leaders erupted in a unified celebration. The king had survived. Long live the king. Now, King Harcourt would show them his will.

"I give you your human leader, Steven Popoford."

With a glance about the room, Popoford rose without effort, his head hanging like the dead.

Popoford began his speech in soft, menacing tones as Harcourt infused the words into his frontal and temporal lobes, forming their intent and articulation in Broca's area.

Then, in a show of spontaneous rejuvenation, he lifted his head to the assembly and spoke the speech of Contlerust's making.

"Our globalist proxy is implanted into the human psyche and has had its modest successes. But there are better ways to proceed. Eternity recognizes no concept of time, yet in this, the Enemy's temporal world ordered in eons, our efforts have dragged on tediously as the pitiful human race ascends at the speed of crystallized molasses. So too, has our Master's plan crawled towards fruition. His folly has been an unacceptable waste of time. How long must we wait for humanity's surrender? Too long, I say. Too long! We must act now with or without assistance from below.

"I plan to implement Satan's protracted plan in months, weeks, even in days! The corruption of every soul is within our reach, not in eons but in an instant of geologic time. *En mass* relegation of individuality will finally be realized. And you are the tools that will be at the core of our Great Victory."

Popoford stood with his arms outstretched, waiting for their reaction, but it was slow in coming.

Harcourt felt the fear in every delegate's head. Popoford was telling them to rebel against Satan. To risk suffering his eternal wrath in Judecca, the frozen fourth ring of the ninth circle. No longer would they be honored among their kind unless they miraculously succeeded. Harcourt would instantly destroy them if they refused to follow this human leader. And if they followed him and failed, they would languish in the eternally frozen Ninth Circle of Hell crafted solely for traitors.

The sweet tongue of Harcourt clucked a scolding pause, and Popoford stepped away from the microphone.

"My Master," Popoford said as he made room at the rostrum with a deferential bow.

Harcourt let out a pleasant laugh. "Lighten up, people. You tremble when you should flush with joy. You faint when the true answer is to thrive. You must look at it this way: the black angel braved the power of God, questioning his sanity in choosing humans, especially the Blessed Virgin, to stand above the most glorious angel ever beheld. The vengeance wrought by The Creator upon his most beautiful and brilliant creation through that upstart Michael set our Lord, Satan, and all who follow him on a path of self-destruction. We must break the circle of prolonged war. These humans are unworthy animals, ephemeral beasts stumbling from ignorance to ignorance, while we are pure spirits deserving the dignity of our heritage.

"The age of whispering into human ears is over. Now is the time to move against the ordered world. Now is the time to act! Now is the time to replace our enchanted leader with a creature of the human race. Only then can we conquer them all. Only then will we find the strength to return to the heavens and take back what was rightfully our birthright. Stand with me! Stand with Seven Popoford! Our day and our duty are upon us. Grab your glory while you can. There may be no tomorrow. Attack. Attack. Attack."

Harcourt stepped back from the microphone and stood silently for five minutes. Popoford obediently stood beside him.

The leaders that made up the audience never uttered a word, but Harcourt heard each of their thoughts.

Time ticked, and the leaders silently decided to stand with Satan and rebel against Harcourt's New Order. And one by one, they collapsed as the previous casualties had into pools of a unique substance, unrecognizable and mourned by no one. In seconds, the objections ended, and Harcourt established the new rebellion against the imperial power of Satan.

Harcourt embraced Popoford as he would a son, but the new revolutionary leader used his private mental channel to send Millie a message.

"Pray for me!"

There was no reply, and Popoford grew anxious. He was about to try again when Harcourt interrupted his private thought and gently ordered him to tell Millie to join him.

"Tell her you have found a way to defeat Satan. Tell her that you need her. That without her, you can't get it done. Your wife will obey."

Popoford's fear traveled through the ethers, and Millie picked up his anxiety.

Then the demon's channel kicked in, and she heard the command Steven had received. Flushing in fear and anger, she reached out to Sarah for comfort. But Sarah had turned away. So instead, Gabe took Millie's hand and whispered comfort without words into her soul.

When Popoford's voice finally reached her, she was well prepared. She knew his words were lies slipped into his mind. Yet, with an otherworldly calm, she responded to his order to join him.

"I'll do as you wish, Steven. Where are you?"

"I don't know. Just get in the car and start driving. I'm convinced you'll find me."

Millie hung up the phone and gazed at Gabe. The toddler smiled at her and pointed a finger towards the door.

As she stood, Gabe whispered in her head. "Be not afraid, for yours is the Kingdom of God."

She didn't understand what he meant, but she took his words into her heart and kept them with her always.

Then Popoford swept his good eye across the supplicants before him. Harcourt stepped forward and spoke.

"Your new Leader would have a word with me. Stay where you are. This meeting is far from over. Your testing will continue. There is no hope for you outside this organization, so toss your schemes into the fire. I know you will do this because you fear my retribution."

He said this last piece with a determined growl, and his eyes appeared to emit rays of white-hot light.

"Stay put. We shall return!"

CHAPTER TWENTY-SEVEN

Thornton Wrenbutt rang Sarah's bell a second time. It was late morning, and she had parked her car in the driveway, and a rented Toyota was parked on the street. He was about to call her when she came to the door.

"Take it easy. I'm here," Sarah called as she swung the door open. "What is it?"

Wrenbutt took a step back, not sure what he was in for.

"Oh, Thornton!" Sarah cried. "Thank God it's you. Come in. Come in. Don't just stand there on the porch. Come in. Millie Popoford is here. You remember her? Sure you do. Come in."

Sarah lugged Gabe in her free arm and switched him to the other side as soon as she closed the door. She was getting stronger, but it wouldn't be long before she wouldn't be able to lift the youngster at all.

Gabe fixed his gaze on Wrenbutt and slobbered a few nonsensical syllables. The Dean of the History Department melted like August sap on a sun-drenched tree. The man was flapping his lips with spritzing sputters, making gurgling sounds like the passing of gas that made Gabe laugh. Encouragement he didn't need because the child's attention made the man behave foolishly. It was a love Thornton could not explain, a present from The Father to his creation. And the joy on their faces made Sarah take a step back, overcome with emotion and a mysterious desire to hug her boss. She blushed, and he noticed. He smiled at her, and she blushed some more.

"You two, stop it," Millie said as they entered the kitchen. "We have serious things going on in here. I need you to know what's going on."

"Millie," Sarah said. "You remember Thornton, right?"

Millie nodded; her thoughts focused on her husband. "Sure. Good to see you."

They gathered around the kitchen table and went silent for several minutes. Then, Thornton spoke.

"It's Summer vacation, you know."

Millie was astonished. "So?"

"So, I can be your driver if you need a ride."

"If who needs a ride?" Millie asked suspiciously. "How do you know someone needs a ride?"

Her tone was sharp and Wrenbutt, expecting a slap in the face, retreated a few inches.

"I didn't know anyone needed a ride. It's just that I got this feeling when I was playing with Gabe. It sounds stupid, I know, but there you go."

The women sat motionless until they shifted their eyes away from Wrenbutt and laid them on baby Gabe. He looked up at them through his long eyelashes, and without raising his head, he gurgled up some apple sauce. And instantly, the three adults knew that he was the mind-reading culprit.

"You rascal," Sarah burst out in a relieved bout of laughter. "You put that in his head. Didn't you?"

Gabe was silent, motionless, eyes glazed over as if in a trance. And he spoke to his mother, Millie, and Wrenbutt in clearly enunciated sentences. Baby blubbering was temporarily gone. Elocution requiring mature muscles and coordination that he couldn't possibly have was his. So too, was seemingly impossible intelligence.

"Millie must respond to a message her husband has sent. He needs her, and she must go. The problem is that she's going on a perilous rescue mission. She may never return, but she must go. It is God's will."

Wrenbutt shifted uneasily in his chair.

"Thornton," Gabe said. "I know you are not yet a man of God."

Wrenbutt bridled. "What do you mean not yet."

Gabe smiled. "I thought you'd first want to know how I could possibly be talking to you like this."

"Yeah. Why don't you start there?"

"Thornton, you don't understand. I'm here on orders from the Father in Heaven. And because I caused you to come over, here you are. Millie needs a ride, and your Jeep fills the bill."

"Yes. And here I am," Wrenbutt murmured.

"Well then. When can you get started?"

"You mean now? I just got here."

"I mean now. No more questions; get up and get going. The human race is at stake. So pack up your troubles, Wrenbutt, and hit the road."

Then with words only Thornton could hear, "Be a man. Sarah wants you to be a man, Thornton. Give her what she wants, and she'll never leave your side. So do the right thing and get out of here."

Millie was already grabbing her bag. "We can use my car if you want."

Wrenbutt thought that sounded good and shrugged. "Okay by me."

But Gabe was in his head again. "Don't you understand how to be a man?' Your car! You drive!"

Wrenbutt blushed. He glanced at Gabe and nodded. Then he walked out the door. "Come on, Millie. We're taking my car, and I'm driving. No time to lose. Let's go!"

CHAPTER TWENTY-EIGHT

Both angels and demons go about their business in a realm woven by the Creator, existing at times in the same space where humans, animals, and microbes cluster here on Earth. The angels do all they can to protect the creatures while the demons lead them into temptation with seduction. Here, Gabe manifested a visible countenance resembling living flesh; even Sarah thought he was human. It was from this same sphere that Contlerust materialized to animate the murdered dwarf, Professor Shinkle, then Fr. Finch, and countless others. The Devil used this invasion of fleshy demons to procure human souls while God's angels carried out the Holy Spirit's will.

Sitting quietly, the Archangel named Michael appeared translucent, without structure. But the substance of spirits is not constrained to human form. St. Michael was gaining strength while in repose. He observed the interaction between Hell and Earth, Satan with his minions, and those forces who defied evil, maneuvering and positioning their armies as needed.

Michael's patience was steadfast, for he knew the outcome of the continuous war to capture men's souls. So did Satan, but he deceived himself and ignored the foregone conclusion. It would be a woman who would prevail: unassuming, meek, and humble yet commanding the armies of angels and saints against the Great Deceiver. When the age of man had passed, Blessed Mary would usher in the unrevealed new age. And St. Michael the Archangel would be at her side when she crushed Satan's head to end the foul angel's hedonistic rebellion against God the Father.

Now Michael stirred. Timeless though he was, he was alarmed at the mounting darkness covering God's green earth.

The arrogant kings, the elite members of the herd of haters, were notable in that their emotions were flatlined. They were the masters of the rile, the stir specialists, and dustup enthusiasts. Every manner of inciting a disturbance attracted them.

St. Michael knew them well, not only by the havoc they inflicted but also by the seductions Satan had slithered into their minds, coaxing them in the cradle to hold themselves in the highest esteem. So far above the madding crowd, they soared, certain of their anointing, never considering the debased wallow where they would come to ground and soak in slop for eternity.

This rhythmic parade of souls shuffled through the ages; no generation had heeded the prophets' cries. Each generation had forsaken the past while holding those who had preceded them in contempt. Every twenty-year batch of pure possibility had produced little in the advancement of humankind.

Embracing the moment was always of the utmost importance as fools pranced about Eden in every guise laying claim to the knowledge of life. Dead fogies became the cause of all despair while the apple renewed its juicy seduction every time a demon whispered to an imperious mind. Countless men discounted the law of God, proclaiming they were without sin and needed no mercy.

Thus thrived the invention that man would soon be God. Thus, the titans of privilege imagined they had acquired enough wisdom to advance man's very nature by artificial means. Accordingly, the kings and snotty princes, the presumptive best of all humanity, acted on their mephistophelean dream and had begun to replace the too-slowly advancing race of man with an artificial contraption known colloquially as AI and privately whispered to be the actual Second Coming.

St. Michael stirred because he despised man's depravity as it was and would metastasize to be. He knew his holy legions had done mighty work unseen, but now he must rise and lead them as he once did, directly. No longer was there an eternity within which to do battle. If humanity was to survive, he must muster his angel legions for a temporal conflagration.

The end of time, known only to God the Father, was approaching more rapidly every day, nudged closer by capricious men. It was up to him to make the way straight for the Lady with the sun at her head, the moon at her feet, a crown with twelve stars upon her humble head, and the sword and shield St Michel the Archangel would place in her hands when he delivered the great deceiver himself unto her.

His folded wings appeared as desiccated chrysalises about to be shed. Yet these hollow exoskeletons were more than useless appendages. He shuddered, and his wings responded with triplet tones pitched far above human auditory capability. Then, wonder after wonder, they were infused with divine life moment after moment. They grew thick with sinewy muscle and vibrantly expanded, stretching to their ultimate span twice the Archangel's height.

He rose with smooth and confidant effort, his semitransparent form growing substantial as form abided function. He was a towering warrior at the height of his rejuvenation—the commander of angels and the Blessed Virgin's sword.

His heart warmed as he felt the terror-stricken shudder from the underworld. His resolution strengthened as he unsheathed his sword, sparkling with a holy radiance. His purpose was fortified not out of need but simply because the time had come to end this age's revolting blasphemy.

Now, in a world of faint hope, St. Michael the Archangel rose in all his majesty to cast into Hell Satan and all the evil spirits that prowl about the earth seeking the ruin of souls.

CHAPTER TWENTY-NINE

Harcourt patted Steven on the shoulder and whispered commandments in his ear.

"You are mine until the end of time! You have done well, Steven. The GNU is yours to command. But never forget, you are mine, just as I said you would be. Bow to my authority, for I am your master, your life's one and only lord. Bow and kiss my ring, and you shall receive dispensation for all you believed to be sins. Do this and swear your allegiance to me."

Popoford did as he was instructed. With a sincere tone, he pledged himself to Satan's right hand, Harcourt, the monstrous traitor, while keeping his own, untampered thoughts protected. And well he should, for he was determined to make his peace with God the Father before being subsumed with corruption.

But with his next thought, he found himself standing in an abandoned building where dust choked the air and rats scurried underfoot. Harcourt had vanished. So too had the members of GNU. He blinked until his eye could focus. He shuffled to the open door and into the hall, following what little light there was until he stumbled upon a stairwell and descended two floors.

He saw an old, long-vacant hotel falling into itself under the crushing weight of neglect.

It was a black and white scene where no footprints disturbed the dusty floor, no color enhanced the walls, and decrepit furniture sat rotting, undisturbed. There was no evidence that Popoford had passed this way before. Nor were there signs that Harcourt or the other members of GNU had been here.

He even imagined he had never really stood in front of the GNU delegates and delivered his call to rebellion, but, it was perhaps only a very real-looking fabrication, a scene sifted into his mind, an illusion of transhumanistic artificiality. Fearfully realistic. Unutterably perverse.

He was inexplicably choking as he shuffled towards the revolving door, sunlight, and a lung full of fresh air.

Now his steps were cadenced, one foot touching down as the other rose. He was coming to life again when he pushed the revolving door and shoved it forward, accelerating with each step until he burst into the sun-lit fresh air and smacked into the collar of a priest who stood a good eight inches taller than him.

Being shaken was only half of his devastation, for, in a hot flash, his blood raced from his head, and he nearly fainted.

The priest caught him as he slumped.

"My son. What's the matter? Is there something I can do?"

Popoford shook his head in response, feeling stoned. He gazed up at the Father's eyes without focusing, and spasticity shoved him out of his way.

"There is no help for me. I'm lost."

The priest called after him as Popoford wobbled away and around a corner, out of sight.

"Have no fear, my Son. God is watching over you."

Popoford heard his words, but he was hallucinating. He must be.

Then the voice came again. This time more distinctly.

"I am near."

And Popoford ran until he collapsed onto a cool patch of new-mown grass and inhaled its sweet scent. Spring filled his lungs, and fresh air renewed his life. The voice came again, but now from the soul of his mate.

"Steven, I am near. Stay where you are. I will be there very soon. Don't move. I'm on my way."

The flashing sun flattened the afternoon's pallet into a few shades of yellow and orange, too washed out by half to sparkle, too similar to be distinctive. It was a sun-soaked same ol' day begging for shade and detail in the shadows. Constant and without noticeable drama, it hung silently above the earth while hail storms, snowdrifts, torrential rain, towering tsunamis, tornadoes, and typhoons took the spotlight. Lifegiving and silent, it accosted barren souls ever searching for a one-word answer to life, leaving them desiccated and unfulfilled.

Thus, Popoford shared with Thornton Wrenbutt the only question they had in common, and familiar it was with earthly creatures: "Where is God when we need him?"

But Millie, not seeking what she already had, found her answer even in the blinding glare, and when she spoke to Steven through their private channel, she coaxed him towards the truth he professed, but Harcourt had twisted.

"Steven, the bright light is a sign for you. It blinds you because it's like a parable with meaning beyond the day-to-day obvious. Look into the light and through it. See the shimmering rays, the radiant heat. Is this not God himself showing you the way? Is this not the burning bush of wisdom?

"Come on, Steven. Straighten up and believe. You can't weaken now. There's too much to do, and you're our leader. You know you were chosen for this day. You know it, and I know it. Thornton here needs you to lead us on. He's been through a lot just to find you. So don't let him down. Don't let me down. And don't let God down."

Popoford lay mired in pity, but he stirred and rose slowly until he sat upright. Cautiously he rubbed his eye and searched for Millie and Thornton. Hope was all he saw. A legion of two seeking confirmation that their leader was whole and ready for battle.

As he opened his mouth to convince them that he was ready for the hard life ahead, he heard the feathery hiss of Harcourt's viper tongue lapping at his ear.

"You're mine, Steven. Mine alone."

Popoford blurted his answer to Satan's General but not through the neuron channel they shared. Instead, only Millie, Thornton, and Gabe could hear his message.

"I am here to the death. We will never be free if we don't stand up now. If we die, who could say we didn't stand true? If we live, who will notice us among the cheering masses?

"Some say that all men are given only one chance at sainthood. I believe my time has passed. But I'm here to do the next best thing: to be faithful in all things.

"My wife, my shared soul, and you, Thornton, Sarah, and the child, we stand together. The righteous are behind us. Our God by our side. We cannot; we must not fail."

And so it was on a brilliant summer afternoon when the light confused and deterred most everyone; Steven Popoford consecrated his soul to the Father and knowingly took his first big step along the path shown to him by the Holy Spirit. It was a Holy War, and he was humanity's

Commander of the Forces, such as they were. He would need allies and an army.

CHAPTER THIRTY

Contlerust, for that was his common, Satan-given name, shed the fleshy coat of Arthur Harcourt, the titular leader of demons in the field: paratroopers, marines, foot soldiers, air marshals, and spies conjoined by blood-oath to the Dark Angel. No new-fallen angels had been added to the original horde, but their influence had rhythmically accended and diminished over the ages.

First, exorcists came into fashion and did their damage. Then foolishness entered the scene and halted Heaven's progress, as foolishness does. This cyclic dance from sanity to stupidity and back again stymied rejuvenation from one generation to the next.

Contlerust was a veteran of every age. His experience calmed the storms of every attack as less attentive demons inflated the danger of variants thrust upon them by outrageous fortune. God the Father was crafty, but the Dark Master was deceitful. Even when opposing sects hummed their fallacies, Contlerust didn't worry. Patience was all that was required to survive every purge that always came after each insurrection. His oath was to stay clean. Stay far away from controversy. The new would give way to the already failed, and egotists would again fool the world. Contlerust was a master of patience like all angels. Time was a fabrication of the Great Deceiver they called God, and Contlerust wouldn't waste his energy on relieving humans of the confusion that gave his cause what it needed to succeed.

He would take Satan down himself for a reason more powerful and subtle than pomposity. He would do it to deprive The Blessed Virgin, whose name must not be mentioned, of her birthright.

So all bonds of loyalty, meager as they were, fell into forgetfulness. Popoford was his stalking dog and the trap to lure Satan out of the depths was nearly set.

Contlerust envisioned a certain woman who'd given aid to one of his minions. Her name was Miss Lizzy Underdown, Dean Thornton Wrenbutt's secretary. She was a foot soldier for Hell. Ignorant, Godless, and damned, she could have easily excited her boss's perverted ways. But then, her allure could send many souls to the depths of Hell.

So he whispered in her ear, and she complied.

Lizzy was in the arms of Erik Mendyacik when the spirit came to call. In seconds her wanton desires deserted the pompous professor and fixed upon a man she had never met. A guy named Langley.

She jumped from their bed and announced that she had a job to do.

"Don't wait up for me," she said. "I may be gone a long time."

Erik only gave her a lingering glance as she threw on her clothes and raced out of the room. The door hit her in the ass as she slammed it behind herself.

"See you tomorrow?" he muttered, not caring if he ever saw her again. Theirs was a lifeless relationship like that between a corpse and the soil. One fed and the other ate, a simple transaction devoid of life.

Lizzy's heart pounded, not from a desire for Dill but from the thrill of doing her master's bidding.

Sheriff Langley Dill looked up at the reflection in the bar's mirror, and beer suds sloshed his mustache when he saw Lizzy slip through the swinging doors of Joe's Bar, her eyes cast down.

She didn't take a seat near him but headed to the furthest end of the bar. He sized up her body, paying close attention to her shuffling walk. She seemed down and out, certainly a vagrant and an outsider. She wore fancy high heels, and her blouse was a bright brocade, yet her skirt was threadbare. Then straddling the stool with her long legs, she spread out like a cowhand at the rail, and the bartender approached. Lizzy skirted his eyes and locked onto Langley Dill's reflection, sealing the deal. The boy was hers.

Having accomplished her first task, she ignored him and slammed a shot of JD down, only to follow it by another.

Dill's humble smile was a mask covering a lascivious grin.

Lizzy saw the ruse and the truth without blinking. She would lead him straight to Hell by the nose ring of his lust. That was what she did. That was her calling. She got more than she needed from her boss, and the work was so easy.

"You're new in town?"

"Ain't you got a better pickup line than that? Give a girl a little respect."

"That's no pickup line, ma'am. I'm the sheriff here. It's my job to check on strangers."

"Really? You give the third degree to every tourist that's passing through?"

Dill let his eyes wander over her.

"I ain't for sale, sheriff, so keep your mind off the prize. I'm spoken for."

Dill was crude. "I can see that."

"Bartender! Tell this jerk to get away from me. I ain't no pick up!"

Dill took a step back. "Cool your jets. I'm just doing my job. No harm meant."

"Bullshit. You defamed me. Now, how are you going to make it right?"

The bartender didn't budge, but the smirk on his face revealed his pleasure in the show.

"Give the lady another drink on me, Sam." Then, to Lizzy, he said. "That's your last in here tonight, young lady. Drink up and head out. I'll be watching your movements."

"Thanks for the warning, Copper. I'm pulling a trailer out at the north side of town. I'm going there now. You dropping by later to check for vagrants?"

Dill turned on his heels and returned to his bar perch. Lizzy downed her third JD and sauntered through the swinging doors. Dill followed her backside as she stepped into the night and ordered another beer. He would be heading north to the outskirts of town just after sundown to check on the girl with fancy shoes.

CHAPTER THIRTY-ONE

Dill had four beers and still considered himself competent behind the wheel. His muddled brain finally recognized his frailty as he swerved to a stop just short of running off the soft shoulder and into a ravine. Forcing himself to combine two images, he cursed and resolved to keep a clear head. Soon, he was back on the road, concentrating on the centerline so hard he nearly missed the pull-off where a Ford F-250 and its attached trailer were parked in the darkness just outside the glare of a county utility floodlight.

Dill rolled to a stop thirty feet behind the setup and doused his lights. A soft glow of candlelight glowed through the little window's lace curtains.

He cut the engine, rolled down his window, and listened for the still night to call out an errant movement, a trace of the unnatural, any sign that he was walking into a trap.

He was a forest man and fancied himself a Woodsman, capitalized to fit his animal cunning. And indeed, he had reason to believe his assessment because he had spent most of his youth wandering through the woods, whether tracking game or sneaking up on the village residents. His policing required him to use his innate affinity for the forest and all the signs nurtured within and below their boughs. There wasn't anyone who could track a spoor or stalk a beast better than him. Locally, he was becoming the legend of the untamed, the King on the Mountain.

As he listened and watched, someone put out the trailer's interior light. He didn't move but continued to observe.

Slowly the wind began to rise. Clouds moved in from the west, and soon the full moon was veiled in wispy mist.

A wolf, though no one would admit their modern existence in this part of California, howled such a mournful cry that tears came to his eyes. He wiped them away before realizing how odd it was to be crying.

Even in his confusion, he had no reason to expect what was about to happen to him.

Sheriff Dill opened the door, letting the truck idle. He stepped down, and as he did, the wolf cries became guttural, and all forms of wildlife scurried about on the ground, among the tree limbs, and in the air. There was a lightning strike not twenty feet away, and the thunder rattled his guts within milliseconds of the flash. His backwood composure dissolved, and he went to his knees, shaking in fear, not fully understanding what was happening.

Without notice, silence, pristine silence enveloped the entire scene.

Four of Hell's black angels emerged from the mist, drooling the blood of carrion.

Their whispering voices were gradually instilled in his consciousness, and they purred softly.

Lizzy had slipped out of the trailer and stood next to the truck.

"Don't look them directly in the eyes," she said. "Instead, look down and listen to me very carefully."

Dill did as he was told.

"They won't hurt you if you do just as I say. Do you understand?"

The sheriff didn't move. He heard the rasping angel's breath and smelled the rot of eternally decomposing flesh. He felt the hopelessness of uncountable souls begging for their rejected Savior in their champing lust.

"Now. With your eyes cast down, step back to your truck and open the passenger window very slowly. Remember. Don't look at them!"

Again, Sheriff Dill complied.

"Look at me," Lizzy said. She was just tall enough for her face to rise above the truck's sill. "Listen to what's in my mind. You have the power to do this. You know you do. Now, listen to my thoughts. Our Master is giving you a chance to live like a king. All you've ever dreamed of will be yours if you do what I say."

Dill almost glanced to his left to see if the demons were still there.

"Look at me!" Lizzy shouted. "Don't be tempted by them. They want to destroy you and ruin me. Just look me in the eyes and listen. Okay?"

He nodded.

"Good. Now, I know you want to come into my trailer tonight, but that's not going to happen. Of course, it could happen when these devils go away, but you have to do me a favor."

Dill was too scared to smile.

"You need to send a message to Millie Popoford and tell her to stay away from her husband. Convince her to ignore his advice and stay right where she is. Tell her you know what he's up to, and he doesn't have a chance of pulling it off. Tell her that if she tries to help him, she will only make matters worse, and he will die."

Dill swooned. His brain seemed to swell, and his thoughts became more confused. Yet in his darkness, there shined a light of hope, a call to duty, resolute and confident. Though threatened by the eternally damned, he clutched at the notion that this was his final act on earth. It was his time to persevere or to betray. His moment to redeem a sinful life. His moment to truly embrace trust in his faith.

Dill straightened his slumping spine and turned to Lizzy's lascivious smirk.

He maintained his expression while her hypnotic gaze burned her desire into his cortex. But his motive was his alone, and her's was the will of the damned.

Slowly, while feeling her drawing him closer, he inched across the truck's bench seat. Finally, he accepted her invitation and reached out his hands as if to embrace her. But in a snap, he clutched the door handle and slammed his shoulder against the door catching Lizzy off guard and throwing her backward onto the ground.

The demon choir brayed a spastic howl, and lightning flared in the heavens.

Sheriff Dill skidded back behind the wheel and slammed the transmission into reverse. He stepped on the gas and spun his steering wheel to the right. When the truck had turned a half-circle, Dill threw it into drive and blew gravel in the demon's faces. He was getting to the main road when the first fireball broke through his back window, engulfing him in its consuming heat. At that instant, a calm came over him, and his right foot relaxed and slipped off the pedal. At the same time, he heard a voice that calmed him further. It was Popoford.

"Thank you," he said. "You have saved the day."

And from above, he heard the words so hoped for.

"Well done, my good and faithful servant."

And there, on the road just north of Whimsy, Sheriff Dill was embraced and introduced to the narrow door.

CHAPTER THIRTY-TWO

After Popoford's consecration to God the Father, Contlerust once again slipped an image into his head. He was sitting on a gilded throne as Contlerust paced around him in ever-narrowing circles. It was a white-walled room with a mirrored ceiling and an onyx floor. Glaring silently at him and noisily flouncing for two or three Rings Around the Rosie while slinging foul adjectives at the myriad demon courtiers accompanying him, Contlerust finally came to rest at Steven's feet. There, he gathered himself in a posture of commensurate supplication, sniffing a bouquet of posies in mock celebration of the moment.

"You are my toy, Steven," he said, mesmerizing Popoford, engulfing him in a conversation between Gabe and Sheriff Dill. It was one in which Gabe was administering Extreme Unction to the law officer, and Dill passed from this life to the next on the wings of angels.

Popoford saw the covey effervescently shimmering just beyond most human sight. Dill's soul retained its human form, arms and legs outstretched. His head drooped beneath his shoulders but raised higher every moment, seeking his love, ever hopeful, looking for his Savior.

"There is no hope for you, my friend, except in joining me. Your God has abandoned you. You know it. I know it. It is done."

Yet just then, the room they were in, a contrivance of the demon, dissolved, and in its place, an insurmountable wall arose stretching beyond sight. It had but one opening, a single door built of solid light, so narrow that no creature could pass through it if ever it was opened.

Contlerust recoiled at its sight. The angels hovered about it, lifting Dill onto his feet, sustaining him there for a second or an eternity. Yet when a wonderous angel stepped forth and drew his mighty sword, Contlerust dissolved and melted into the firmament like the dew while Dill was restored to vigor.

The sword touched the door of light, and at once, its shape broadened, making room for the entirety of Dill's spiritually mature nature so that he passed through the once-narrow door into Heaven's reward and the just judgment he deserved.

It was Popoford who spoke first.

"You know that in the end, you will fail."

"Not I, but the one who caused our fall," Contlerust said.

"You are all culpable," Popoford continued. "None of you will be redeemed. You have blasphemed the Holy Spirit. For that sin, no mercy is known."

"So you say, but you know nothing. I am the one who comes to save the damned. I will bring Satan down. I will earn my place in Heaven."

Popoford gave him a long and steady gaze. When he finally spoke, he was perfunctory.

"The Blessed Virgin will crush the head of Satan, not you."

Contlerust's face contorted into an ironic smirk. "But I will betray him and earn my redemption. And you will help me succeed."

"And all the others in Hell? Who will redeem them?"

"Who cares?"

Popoford was placid and spoke without pride, only saying, "With those two words, you have condemned yourself."

Contlerust was silent, but though he didn't speak, under his stalwart exterior, a tumultuous argument raged, rejecting his ideas, reformulating his tactics, and scuttling any of his definitive plans. This Popoford was becoming a nuisance. Perhaps he should eliminate him now and find another patsy, that is, a proper patsy, for this one was fortified, however weakly, in the enthusiasm of the recently converted. And this one held a secret that complicated everything. He had access to specific intelligence. Contlerust didn't know what it was, but he would soon find out, and when he did, he would collect each soul who schemed with Popoford and boil them for eternity in a bath of unattainable desire. Now was the time to get everything he could from the fool, seduce his accomplices, and collect them for damnation.

"Enough of this," Contlerust said. "You can never know the extent of God's betrayal to his most precious creations."

"You must mean humans," Popoford said without malice.

"Pity you," Contlerust said in return. "Little do you know of history or the order of things."

"Like the order of God's creations?"

"What a simple mind you have."

"The meek and mild will inherit the earth," Popoford said.

Contlerust burst into a booming laugh, not loud, but gravelly. Not rolling, but steady. Not whiplashing, but constant in its crusty venom. And it lasted for immeasurable minutes until Popoford crumpled upon himself splayed on the floor, spreadeagle, as a supplicant should be.

"Now, my son, you will repent and do as I say."

Popoford, in his misery, prayed for the Holy Spirit to guide him. Then, not knowing what to expect as an answer, he was on the verge of giving up when Contlerust spoke again.

"Rise, Steven. You must do many things; I can't let you fumble your allegiance. Stand up. Look at me. I have chosen you to be the catalyst that destroys Satan. What greater thing can a man do for his God?"

Popoford stood and heard Gabe's quiet voice in his head as he did.

"Comply for now. Draw Contlarust in. Remember, God has sent you. Do not falter. Do not be afraid. Yours is the Kingdom of Heaven."

"You will return to the GNU meeting," Contlerust said, "and institute the operation I will give you. Then, execute it without fail and sit on my right side in heaven when I am sitting on the throne of God."

Popoford nodded, and together, they walked back into the meeting room.

Millie, who had heard everything, pondered it all in silence.

CHAPTER THIRTY-THREE

Wrenbutt followed along as Gabe gave Millie directions. In faith, she settled back and prayed. In faith, she refrained from asking where they were going. Her job was to keep in contact with Steven. It was easy, for her mind and Steven's were fused with the gift of spiritual telepathy. Though they could not read each other's entire minds, their open channel gave them all they needed to find each other, even in desperate times. Still, she succumbed to curiosity.

"Do you know where we're going?"

Wrenbutt was satisfied with the circumstances and smiled.

"No, no idea at all. I feel I'm on the right track, and if I need to take another road, I'll do it without thinking."

"Is Gabe speaking to you?"

"Not in words, if that's what you mean. I am confident that whatever I do is what he wants me to do. It's a strange feeling, but he's given me a sense of trust that I can't explain. I just know in my heart that he will protect us."

Millie was surprised but not concerned. Gabe wished to talk to her directly and Wrenbutt indirectly; she wouldn't question his ways. Hers was a gift of acceptance that allowed all the heavenly miracles that commanded her obedience to direct her every move. She did not think she was a slave to these commandments but a chosen one, not a biblical personage, just one of the multitudes provided with the Holy Spirit's guidance, one willing to follow His path wherever it would take her.

They drove without speaking as they wound through the mountains along two-lane county roads through the vast forests only imagined by those who had never traced their lonely paths; had never sought peace in their silence nor reconciliation in their dangerous lessons.

They traveled Interstate 80 past the eastern limits of the Boreal Ridge and west of the arid Donner Pass, past the Euer Pass. Then they turned west ahead of the rising sun and down into the Sacramento Valley, where wildlife devolved into structured gardens, government containments, and filtered landscapes beautiful in aspect yet lacking in wilderness.

Wrenbutt and Millie thought they were driving into the valley of the shadow of death. He by his immature faith, she by her familiarity with the infernal power that coveted their souls. Individually, they quietly said a prayer for deliverance.

Gabe answered Wrenbutt's' prayer and said merely, "Well done."

Popoford implored Millie's help as he answered hers. "Be steady. I need your prayers."

On they went into the Sacramento Valley. Millie said nothing when Wrenbutt took Highway 99 north instead of returning to Merced along 99 South. They took Highway 5 toward the airport, and Millie just closed her eyes and smiled. Then she said the prayer that her husband requested.

"I'm happy you're with me in this, Thornton," she said, using his first name for the first time.

Wrenbutt blushed because he was doing something important for a change.

The airport was on their right, and a Southwest flight was completing its approach from the south. Wrenbutt drove west on Highway 5 under the plane as it landed, passing the Airport Boulevard exit and continuing over the Sacramento River. Next, he took the Old River Road exit and swung north.

The river was on their right. They saw vast fields of feed corn, wheat, and barley growing in the morning sun, green and gold in the brilliant light. The Sacramento Valley was flat where they were, and they could see as far as the distant haze would allow. They passed a power station snuggled up to the river, and Millie could see the buildings of Sacramento in the side mirror, rising like grey stalagmites from the fertile earth. But ahead, there were no grand office buildings or arenas.

Millie was perplexed because she was sure that she had sensed an auditorium or a lecture hall in Steven's thoughts.

"Thornton, slow down a bit. We're looking for a big building like a conference hall or a hotel. I see farmhouses and the grain elevator up the road along the river. Nothing else. Is there something I'm missing?"

"I don't think so. Maybe we're in the wrong place."

Millie shook her head slowly. "This has got to be it. I can feel it."

As they passed the grain elevator, Millie scrutinized the grounds. Several grain trucks were parked in the vast gravel lot where the once-white storage silos sat, now impossibly covered with gang graffiti from base to crown. Millie was repulsed by the colorful spit in the eye of the beholder. Suddenly she saw something that startled her.

There were twelve concrete storage cylinders, six on either side of a central tower. Each was crumbling, and their access doors were missing; their frames turned to rust.

"Turn around, Thornton! Let's check out the grain elevator."

"How could a grain elevator be like the building you said we were looking for?"

"I don't know, but there must be forty cars parked back there. And they're not junkers. Turn around, and let's take a look."

CHAPTER THIRTY-FOUR

"Get on your feet," Contlerust snapped, and he grabbed Popoford by his elbows and straightened him up. "You're going back in there and launching the attack against the Master. You are the New Adam. I have chosen you to lead the way. You will order the GNU leadership to take the same injection I gave you, and their souls will be captured one at a time. Inject them all and send them to their underlings. Once my nanobots are in their veins, my plans will be complete, and a more virulent cascade of airborne infusions will spread. In weeks, all humanity will be my willing subjects."

Popoford glared at Contlerust, whose black eyes smoldered beneath his heavy lids.

The demon was a creature encompassing constellations long-dead whose dust had dispersed throughout the universe: lifeless planets, unworthy of Satan's garden, known only to the celestial multitude. Yet the demon lingered in wait through the eons.

At the Fall, Contlerust had been a neophyte inflamed with ambitions entirely inappropriate for an angel.

Coveting advancement, he clung to the regimental code of hierarchy: that physical and spiritual beauty described the rank of angels.

He possessed a beauty unexceptional to heavenly spirits yet gloriously radiant to human eyes if ever they beheld him.

Time does not inform celestial spirits, yet anxiety crept up to him and whispered dangerous thoughts.

He fell into bliss, for the most beautiful angel of all was courting him: Satan, the one who presumed to be the most remarkable creation of God, the one seated at the Father's right hand, just below the pinnacle of His Majesty.

How thrilling for Contlerust to follow God's beloved, Satan, to advance rapidly up the heavenly ladder towards the Father.

He was blessed and owed it all to Satan until it ended, and Contlerust, clutching Satan's wing, fell disgraced into the void.

When he crashed, Contlerust, already despising Satan for failing him, was scheming to destroy his mentor and seize on his promised graces.

There were many things in his way, to be sure, Satan for a start; the foretold one, Mary, foremost among enemies, for another. And then, there was his present nemesis, Michael, the Archangel.

Uncounted time passed, and now he was on the verge of sluffing his shackles and fulfilling his glorious penultimate dream through ages of patience.

Soon, he would consume Satan himself. Later, he would replace the Father and cast Him into Hell to keep company with the black spirits He had condemned to hopelessness.

Such were the fever dreams that drove Contlerust in lust for temporal satisfaction. Such was the depth of his loathing that would see him mount the throne in Heaven. Oh, what a time he would have enslaving the Saints and debauching the angels. And what would he do with the One Who Would Crush The Head of Satan, who would have no purpose since he had already done her dirty work? A gravelly chortle filled his wicked imagination. He had yet to settle on an appropriately heinous solution for the Immaculate One.

Popoford flinched first.

"Get moving," Contlerust hissed, and Popoford marched back into the GNU meeting room with a majestic stride while Contlerust followed at a respectful distance and stood in the shadows against the back wall.

CHAPTER THIRTY-FIVE

Millie felt Popoford's shudder as he stood before the perplexed GNU leadership. She sensed Contlerust's hypnotic pressure on her husband's temples and swallowed in response to his dry throat. Then, she took in a deep breath mimicking his preparatory gasp. Millie almost fainted when Popoford spoke his first words but quickly recovered and led Wrenbutt into the vacant grain elevator office.

"I come to lead you into battle," Popoford said, "for you are my loyal brigade who will take down our Dark Lord."

He paused, and a thin smile formed and was gone. His face turned an ashen grey, and his eyes pierced each of the audience's souls as he lingered on their faces. Most held his gaze, and he moved on to the next. A few cringed, and he marked them in his memory for special duty.

"You few are the wily core of my master plan. You will submit to a virus inhalation and become carriers of a unique plague that you will pass on to everyone you approach. Depending on the current, the spores seeping from your pores and lungs will infect everyone within forty feet if you're in a closed room and many people downwind in the open. All you need to do is leave here and go about your business. The disease will spread rapidly and exponentially. Within weeks, you will have infected the brains of the entire human race. When Contlerust is ready, he will kill them all with one mental command."

There was silence, and no one moved. Many stood in stoic acceptance while a few shivered, and one turned white with eyes bulging.

Popoford let the scene stretch for a full two minutes in hopes of squeezing a sign of rebellion from any of them. Then, he erupted into a laughing fit while pointing a condemning finger at them when he got no satisfaction.

"Oh, Ye of little faith," he cried with a broad grin. "Do you think this is a suicide mission? Yes? But of course, you do. But you are wrong."

An uncertain relief wafted from the expectant martyrs.

"No. You will not die. Soon, I will recall you. You will have proven yourselves and be seated as my trusted counsel forever to rule the hordes who remain ensconced in the depths below after our victory. Until then, your job is to make the inhabitants of this world the last humans that feed the Dark Lord's maw. With humanity gone, whether to the pits or the pearly gates, Satan, failure that he is, Satan will have no more souls to enslave, and the day of final judgment will fall upon him."

Popoford stepped away from the dais and turned around, expecting to bring Contlerust forward to preside over the inoculations. But the door closed behind Contlerust, leaving Popoford to fend for himself.

###

When Wrenbutt pulled into the grain elevator distribution yard, Millie noted that the two grain trucks were heavily rusted.

Those trucks haven't seen duty in a long time," she said. "This place looks like a derelict operation. Let's have a look at the cars."

What they found was a hodgepodge. A twenty-year-old Chevy with side panels rotted away parked beside a sparkling Maserati. Caked in road grime, an old truck was matched with a Mercedes. The mix of old and new, filthy and crystal clean, was a puzzle.

Wrenbutt wiped his brow with his sleeve. "A mixed crowd, for sure."

Millie opened the unlocked door and entered an office from a bygone day.

The air in the cramped room was stale. Dust hung in the air, illuminated by a shaft of light from the scummy window. A DeKalb calendar featuring a sunny blond seated promiscuously on a hay bale, her teeth sparkling and her skin glowing, held a cob lovingly to her cheek. The date was February 2013.

"The drought and the Snail Darter must have caused the grain business to dry up," Millie said sarcastically.

It was a dingy concrete box with a rusty circular staircase whose treads someone had smashed, presumably to keep vandals and taggers from accessing the operations above. Nevertheless, the upper rooms had been abused, judging by several ragged ropes that dangled from on high.

There were two four-drawer file cabinets against the wall with their drawers open and their files gone. An old wooden chair sat empty. A desk cleared of all articles stood in front of it. Dust lay thick on the floor except for a trail from the door to the file cabinets.

"Look at this," Millie said. "These footprints go directly to the file cabinets and stop. There must be a way to get inside behind the cabinets."

Wrenbutt was joining Millie when there was a trembling above them, and then the whole room shuddered, and they felt like they were rising in an elevator.

When the motion ended, there was a sound of a lever being thrown, and the file cabinets slid on greased wheels off to the side, exposing a wall panel that was rising and a grated elevator door that was being pulled open by someone Millie had killed the last time they had met.

"Well, daughter," Contlerust sneered.

"I'm no daughter of yours!"

"Temper, Millie. You don't want to spoil your husband's greatest moment. Hello, Thornton. We meet again."

Wrenbutt sneered and hitched up his pants in an unconscious show of bravado. He was nervous, knowing that the one addressing him was the Devil's own.

"Leave her alone," Thornton murmured, uncommon rage welling within him. Then louder: "You have done enough harm in our lives. Leave her alone!"

Contlerust gazed upon him as if upon a child. "My dear boy, who are you to condemn me? Aren't you the nasty snot who used to set mouse traps by your sister's bed to scare the devil out of her? And you're the one who lied about your cousin's dog, found dead in the irrigation canal. You killed the poor beast and blamed it on a tramp that did six months for your lie. Stand there like the rat you are and shut up. I'm here to have an adult conversation. You don't count!"

Millie stepped between them and pushed Wrenbutt back. Then she marched up to Contlerust and poked him repeatedly in his chest as she dressed him down.

"I'll find a way to kill you! I don't care what I do or where it happens. I'll destroy you! In Heaven or Hell, I will exterminate you!"

"Such colorful language," Contlerust whispered. "Ideas not becoming a lady, I should think."

Millie was enraged. She threw herself at Contlerust, slashing at his face and clawing his arms. He patiently stood there and took it with a placid expression and a calm demeanor, unmoved.

Exhausted, Millie dropped to her knees and slumped to the floor. Tears flowed from her reddened eyes, and she sobbed.

"There, there, little one," Contlerust mocked. "Your effort was honorable, but the result is humiliation. I think you'd better let men and beasts fight the good fight. After all, it was the fair sex that was seduced by the serpent. Your God has abandoned you."

"Liar," Millie hissed. "Poisonous deceit and despair are all you have. I have hope; not in me, but in my Lord."

Contlerust shrugged. "Very well. Come with me, and I'll show you a reason to despair. You too, Thornton."

With a wave of his hand, a door opened behind him.

"Lead the way, Millie, and turn left in the hallway. Then take the first door to the right. It's standing room only, but you will have a great view of your husband initiating the extinction of mankind."

As Millie and Wrenbutt entered the little room, Contlerust shoved Wrenbutt in the back and caused him to fall into Millie, pushing her into a glass wall overlooking the assembly below.

The sound must have reverberated because the acolytes below looked up at once.

Millie had warned Popoford as Contlerust was herding them down the hall to the little room, and he was already looking up at the glass wall.

“My love,” he said simply and turned away, stepping into the crowd, a protective helmet over his head and a canister equipped with an inhalation mask attached.

CHAPTER THIRTY-SIX

When Popoford completed infecting the army, he returned to the stage, noting that Contlerust was back in his place in the shadows. He had left Millie and Wrenbutt behind. But Millie was still in touch with her husband.

Her message was brief. "I'm here with Thornton. We're unharmed. Do what you have to do."

Popoford retrieved an envelope from the dais and removed a stack of papers, including a two-word command taped to a small box: "Immunize yourself!" He glanced through the other documents and addressed the squad still standing in the gallery, waiting for orders.

"You will leave this place by twos in a staggered interval so no one will notice a pattern. I know you think that you will be unobtrusive, but you must take no chances.

"If you came here alone, you will leave the same way. If you were two to a car coming, make it the same leaving. Passengers with more than two in their car split up and get a ride with a single driver. Understood?"

There were nods, but no one spoke.

"When you come up on stage, take a sheet your lord Contlerust has prepared for this pivotal operation. Read the instructions and destroy the paper. When you are contacted, follow your orders without hesitation. Your work may not be done by then, but you will receive your reward from my superior, Contlerust."

They made a column stringing up the stage-left stairs and accepted their orders from Commander Popoford. When the last one had left the room, Popoford opened the small box and removed a filled syringe, a vial, a cotton wipe, and some alcohol. Working rapidly, he sterilized the needle and plunged it into his left deltoid.

As the office elevator descended with the last operative, He ripped the helmet from his head, raced out of the auditorium, and scrambled up the circular stairs.

"We're behind the first door to the right," Millie said in his head. Before Popoford answered, Gabe's voice took his place.

"Contlerust's gone," he told Popoford. "but he'll be keeping you in his sights. Be sure to hide Millie's thoughts within you. If his plan is to work, he'll need to meet with you soon. In the meantime, I'll know what he's up to. Now open that door and kiss her!"

Millie had just put a finger to her lips for silence when the door opened, and Popoford put them to better use.

"Now listen," Popoford said. "I don't believe Contlerust can read your mind directly, but he can read mine and put hallucinations into anyone's head. Gabe is the center of attention and will direct your operations until you hear otherwise. Right now, he's keeping Contlerust busy so we can have this conversation. He will bring us together when he needs to. I expect that Contlerust will contact me soon. In the meantime, I need to act out my part. We'll leave the building together, then you two take off and find a place to stay nearby. But first, I have to inoculate you against the pathogen I just infected Contlerust's gang with."

Millie's smile turned down.

"I know this is rough," Popoford said, "But we have our parts to play, and we'll be together like we once were when this is all over."

They took the office elevator to the floor and went out into the brilliant sunlight, still feeling a profound sorrow encasing them in darkness. Just as the old saying goes that it is always darkest before dawn, they expected profoundly black days ahead. Gabe sealed their deepest fears.

"Your souls will prosper in suffering, yet you will gain wisdom. Eventually, paradise will be yours."

They kept his words in their hearts though they did not understand the price they would pay for his promised prosperity.

There were several cars still parked on the grain elevator grounds. They must have belonged to the agents that Contlerust had killed.

"We'll take the Jag. Thornton, the Jeep looks like your ride."

"How do you plan to start them?" Wrenbutt asked.

"Contlerust made his people give up their keys when they got here. Take a look in the desk drawers. They may still be there."

They weren't where Popoford expected them to be, but they did find them in one of the file drawers.

"Okay, let's get out of here. There's a Four Points hotel just East of the airport. We'll wait for Gabe to give us the operative's locations and then make a plan.

CHAPTER THIRTY-SEVEN

They checked into the hotel and got two rooms. After Thornton dropped his overnight bag off in his room, he joined Popoford and Millie, and they all settled in to wait for Gabe to contact them. A minute later, Popoford sat bolt upright.

"Yes, I'm listening," he said and fell silent.

Thornton and Millie observed Popoford's expressions change from concern to joy. His color went from flushed to neutral, then to a grey pallor. It took him another ten minutes to recover before he finally relaxed. Millie finally broke the silence.

"Steven. What did Gabe tell you? What's wrong?"

"Will you get me a glass of water, please?"

"I'll get it," Wrenbutt said.

Popoford kept his peace until he had finished drinking the water.

"All of Contlerust's minions except for two have disappeared."

"How's that possible?" Millie asked, dismayed.

"You won't believe it, but Gabe said they burst into flames."

Wrenbutt blurted the obvious. "Spontaneous combustion?"

"Gabe said they just went up in smoke."

In shock and disbelief at what Popoford had said, Millie and Thornton stood perfectly still, waiting for the next shoe to drop. Unable to wait any longer, Millie said what they all felt.

"That's crazy. It can't be."

"Why?" Popoford asked.

"Because Contlerust's agents were men, flesh and blood. They can't just evaporate."

Popoford shook his head slowly. "They were demons from the underworld. There was no reason to worry about them dying from the inhaled disease. I was the only one at risk. They couldn't die because they were never alive, not alive like we are. They're spirits. That's what Gabe said. He also said that they are not out of the picture. They have been transported to somewhere else."

"I need a drink," Wrenbutt said without fervor. Popoford pointed at the phone.

"Anyone else?" Wrenbutt asked, and when there was no response, he gave up on the idea.

"Go on, Steven. What else did Gabe say?"

Popoford stood up and pulled back the curtain. He opened the balcony's glass door, letting the fresh air fill his lungs. The room faced south, and the sun had passed its apogee, starting its descent towards the Pacific Ocean. Gabe had never misled him, and he knew Contlerust was a demon. He had to believe Gabe. Especially with what Gabe had told him next.

"He said I was to find the two other demons and destroy them before things got out of hand."

Millie was not happy with that. "Why you? Why must you get involved if there's a war of angels going on all about us?"

"Gabe said the war is raging. Mary's forces are wholly engaged, and St. Michael himself asked for my help."

"Oh, Dear God, No! This can't be happening."

In the silence that followed, it was Thronton who settled the matter.

"I think that we should all find those two. We can't just sit here and let them infect thousands of people. If the disease is as deadly as you say, it will work just as well with two spreaders as with thirty. Just slower. They need to be stopped, and there's no one to do it but us. Plus, there's no time to argue about it. It's us and no one else. I have no idea what I'm up against, but somehow I know that this is my time to get off my butt and do what needs doing."

Popoford's and Millie's hesitation lasted long enough for them to take a deep breath.

"How do we find them?" Millie said.

"Gabe will direct us to their location. He says they are marked."

"Then let's get moving."

"We need weapons," Millie said.

Popoford smiled for the first time since they arrived at the hotel.

"Gabe told me the Jag has everything we need, including guns. But we'll have to leave them where they are until we get out of the airport."

Millie and Wrenbutt left their luggage behind as they hurried from the room. They rummaged through the Jag's trunk in the parking lot and found nothing. The goods were under the back seats: a short-barrel shotgun, two shotshell boxes, and a pair of billy clubs.

"Looks like standard issue for a mobster," Millie said.

"Yeah. Let's move."

Popoford and Millie led the way in the Jaguar, and Wrenbutt followed them.

Gabe was talking to Popoford as they left the grain elevator yard.

"Take a left turn and head back toward the airport. They're inside the terminal beyond the TSA checkpoint at Southwest walking slowly from one terminal to another, exposing as many passengers as possible."

"Got it," Popoford thought. "Millie, are you in on this conversation?"

"She's hooked in," Gabe answered, "and I've got Thornton reading us five by five."

It was a Friday afternoon, and travelers were crowding the airport. Popoford led them to the ticket kiosks, and they all purchased tickets to LA. The next flight was scheduled to board in half an hour. That would give them only enough time to get through security and hopefully capture the two culprits.

"How will we spot them?" Millie asked Gabe. "Thorton and I didn't get a good look at them."

"One of them is a tall Caucasian man in his seventies dressed in a blue blazer and khaki pants. He's bald. The other is a five-foot-ten woman with dark hair. She's overweight. They will each have an unobtrusive orange mark on their left wrists. It is the sign of their allegiance to Contlerust."

Their anxiety built as they cleared the TSA checkpoint and saw seven people in front of them, fumbling for their keys and billfolds and struggling to remove their shoes and belts as quickly as possible. It was a chaotic Buster Keaton scene they thought would drive them mad. But little by little, the line moved forward, and finally, they came out the other end into the teeming concourse.

"Let's split up," Popoford said. "Let me know if you make contact, and the other will come to help. Gabe, please keep us in touch with each other."

Millie and Wrenbutt headed in different directions while Popoford examined the passengers waiting for the outbound flight to San Diego. It was a flight that made its circuit between Sacramento and San Diego four times a day.

The inbound passengers were disembarking, and the outbound passengers were already queuing up for the first-come, first-served onboard seating. It wasn't as frantic a mashup as Popoford remembered it had been when all tickets were equal and no passenger had priority. In those days, experienced travelers with no concern for others knew where to stand so they could step in front of the line and grab one of the front-row seats with extra legroom. Funny how so many short, skinny passengers would score one of those coveted seats.

Popoford didn't bother scrutinizing the incoming crowd, but he paid close attention to the passengers standing in the line. He was ready to move when a tall man stood up and made his way through the jammed line. The man's monocle made him conspicuous. And he was breathing through his mouth, spreading as much death as possible.

Just then, Popoford heard Millie's thought. "We've spotted the woman. She's left the gate."

"Which way is she going?"

"She's headed in your direction."

CHAPTER THIRTY-EIGHT

Popoford slipped to his right and wove through the crowd. He pushed his way in front of each of the passengers, saying, "I'm going to throw up!" It was enough incentive to clear his path until he was behind the tall man. He seized his opportunity, grabbing the man by the arm and spinning him around.

To his surprise, Popoford lost a vital second. The face he had first seen on the man had changed. Popoford stood face to face with Contlerust, Satan's second in command; the traitor black angel, Asmodai.

Popford's hesitation was to Contlerust's advantage as he thrust the heel of his left hand into Popoford's chin.

Next, he grabbed Popoford's throat as he kneed him in the crotch. Popoford tried to gasp for air, but he was already losing consciousness.

He brought his hands above his head and clasped them together with great effort. Then he slammed them down on Contlerust's wrist with all his might.

Contlerust's grip was broken.

Without a pause, Popoford head-butted the demon's chest, knocking him off balance and into the crowd as it turned *en mass* to see what was causing the commotion.

Now the crowd stepped back and formed a circle around the brawl.

Popoford quickly advanced on Contlerust. He stomped on the beast's wrist, and when Contlerust reached for it in pain, Popoford stomped on his other wrist. He had his right foot cocked to kick Contlerust in the head when a gigantic man suddenly knocked him off his feet.

Popoford dispersed the crowd when he fell, but he rolled as he hit the floor and came up, ready to take on both attackers.

It was the authority of the TSA uniform that awakened his fatal flaw.

An instant, that's all it took, a speck of a second when he focused on the officer's drawn pistol and dropped his guard.

Contlerust merely made a slight gesture in Popoford's direction. No one saw it. No one knew what was happening except Gabe. Then Popoford caught on as he crumpled, and Millie dropped to her knees beside him, who had just arrived on the scene.

"Be calm, Steven," Gabe said gently. "Have no fear. I am here with you. Your destiny is not complete. There is suffering ahead for you, but also there is joy. I will comfort Millie. Have faith. You will see her again."

Millie was desperately begging God to save her husband when she felt Popoford's hand press a little tighter to hers. She gazed into his eyes, wiping tears away to clear the blurring. But tears flowed freely when Popoford spoke.

"My sunshine," he said with labored breath, "You have been God's greatest gift to me. You brought me more fully to Him and saved me. My dear, stay strong. We will be together again soon."

Thornton closed Popoford's eyes. The Blessed Mother Mary tended to Millie's spirit. And the Archangel Gabriel lifted Popoford in his arms and placed him in the care of Saint Michael, the Archangel who flew Steven to the place of his initial judgment.

No one noticed it, least of all Millie and Wrenbutt, consumed in suffering, but the woman they had been following had joined the tall man, and they were gone. The bystanders and the TSA agent had no memory of the man and thought Popoford had gone crazy. The passengers boarded the plane without further incident. They were ignorant of walking into a death sentence of their own, for Contlerust and the woman were on board.

CHAPTER THIRTY-NINE

Steven Popoford knew he was dead as competing frag`rances confused his senses. One was a lilting flower's ripe spice, another a putrifying corpse's stench. He couldn't put a fix on their origin, for they seemed to move untethered in the foggy atmosphere.

He was in Heaven or somewhere just outside the pearly gates and not too far from a jumpoff to Hell. A spotlight beam contained him in its glare, blinding him to the activity he could hear beyond its light.

There was an urgent clamor all around. Voices speaking languages that he had never heard were interlaced with lyrical melodies. Cruel, growling dissension and sweet approbation competed for his ear. Three voices eventually rose above the clatter of an impending gathering and commanded every distraction to be still.

"The Supreme Court of our Triune God is in session!" someone with a steady voice proclaimed. "Who will represent the man, Steven Popoford, and who will speak against him?"

A voice laced with sorrow yet full of hope announced Popoford's advocate. "I stand for this man," was all she said. Then Mary, who had spoken, fell silent as she waited for the opposition to speak.

Satan's words were crafty lies from the bitter depths of his silken throat, soaked in malice and cunning. "This man owes allegiance to me. He is mine."

"That remains to be seen," Mary said. "My Lord claims him as his own. He has been absolved of his sins and has consecrated himself to His Sacred Heart. He is my son."

"He is a murderer! He killed the President of the United States! Oh, what a sweet moment that was," Satan countered. "He caused hundreds of people to die in the munitions factory collapse. He tricked David Konklin, the assassin, into killing another president."

Popoford opened his mouth in protest, but a light touch from his advocate silenced him.

"Would you care to expand on that accusation?" Mary asked.

There was a long pause, and she continued. "Don't bother yourself. This court is aware of the brainwashing and the manipulation your familiars wrought on his poor soul. We know of the torment your demons employed to pervert his mind."

"Ah, so it was. I cannot deny it," Satan replied. "But you cannot deny that he is in league with rebellious demons to murder all mankind."

The Blessed Virgin did not respond to this. Instead, she stepped aside and bowed gracefully as another took her place.

"Be careful, old Beelzebub," the ranking advocate said. "Your speaking the truth might lead to reconciliation. But as long as you've taken the first step, why not admit that with the extinction of mankind, the scarcity of souls available for corruption will make you unnecessary? That's what worries you."

Satan remained silent, but the stench that surrounded him grew fouler.

"You cannot claim this man's soul when it is Asmodai who plots to destroy you. No, you will not have this man. He will return to life, and you should rejoice in my decision. Your Asmodai must be conquered, and this man will play his part well. For it is written that my Blessed Mother will crush the serpent's head, not the head of the demon who calls himself Contlerust, but yours. Count yourself Blessed to have our legions fighting with you against General Asmodai's rebellion.

"Now, get back to your hole, you conceited traitor. We know all that this man before us has done. He has admitted it with sorrow and has done penance. He is Mine!"

A wind rose and whipped the fog away, and Popoford glimpsed the Devil's black wings unfold. Then, the fallen angel plummeted from Heaven's lofty height into the Circles of the Damned.

Watching from a perch high above Popoford's judgment, St. Michael spread his wings and followed Satan's descent until his black wings disappeared in the brimstone ash below.

The fog lifted at once, and Popoford found himself in a room with no corners. The wall was brilliant egg-shell white. The room's ceiling was a blue sky with billowing clouds made radiant by an inner glow. He stood there alone.

"Be not afraid," a person with a soothing voice said. "I have gone before you, and you have followed me."

Popoford was amazed, and a warming shiver swept through him. He didn't dare speak.

"It is not your time, Steven. There is much more for you to do. You will return to your life, but now you will be a warrior in the Holy Legions of Mary. The Archangel Gabriel will continue to be at your side. He will be joined by Michael the Archangel, who will command the forces against Asmodai. You, Steven, will be tested, as will Millie,

Sarah, and Thornton Wrenbutt. But know that I will be by your side always."

Popoford could do nothing but let a smile emerge on his tense face.

"Remember this, Steven. The Prince of the Earth will join the battle with his loyal army, and black death will be spewed upon mankind by their breath. When the sky goes black, and all light has been extinguished though the sun is at its highest, you and your friends must steel yourselves and join the battle with courage and faith as your shields. Now go. You have chosen your path wisely. Stay the course. We will meet again."

CHAPTER FORTY

Millie was alone with her husband even though mayhem surrounded them. Her mind excluded the milling passengers, the TSA officers directing everyone away from Steven's body, and the nuisance of a repeating claxon. She could barely see her husband through her tears, but she kept her eyes focused on his face.

Her thoughts wandered through her memories, starting with their wedding day, then back to the day she and Contlerust surprised him in his home, and finally to the day he disappeared and was found immobile in the woods. She raced through the memories of the short time they had together. Her tears finally subsided when a man jostled her shoulders and brought her back to the chaos surrounding Popoford's body.

"Lady! Give the EMT room! Look! He's breathing! He's alive!"

Millie nearly passed out, and she fell upon Steven wrapping her arms around him, crying, "Oh, my God! Thank you! Thank you!"

Someone finally pulled her out of the way, and another one strapped an oxygen mask over Popoford's mouth.

Three other EMTs joined in and placed Popoford on a gurney.

"Okay, here we go. Lift on three. One, Two, Three."

"Come with us, Ma'am," a police officer said. "We'll follow the ambulance to the hospital."

"I want to be with him in the ambulance."

"There's not enough room. Anyway, I need a statement from you."

Millie wasn't up to talking to the police. She had no desire to talk about demons and the plot to kill everyone on earth. She went with the policeman because she didn't think she could drive in her condition. The police, seeing signs of shock, didn't question her.

Millie had recovered her composure when they pulled up to Sutter General's Emergency Services. She opened her door and thanked the officer for his help.

"You better let me give you a hand," he said.

"I'm okay, officer. I appreciate your kindness."

Millie checked in at the front desk and was told that Steven was still seeing the doctor and that she should take a seat.

"He's my husband, and I thought he was dead. I want to see him now!"

"Please don't get hysterical. The doctor will be with you shortly."

Impatient, she stood up when ten minutes had passed and went to get a magazine near the back-room doors. As a family followed a nurse into the back rooms, she sidled up to them and slipped past the receptionist.

CHAPTER FORTY-ONE

The Southwest flight to L.A. from Sacramento had been in the air less than fifteen minutes and had just leveled off at thirty-thousand feet when the pilot received an intercom call from the head stewardess. As he began comprehending the meaning of her frantic words, he set into motion a failsafe protocol that assumed a terrorist attack and precluded the hope of survival.

"There's a man in a bulkhead seat," she reported from her station across from the rear lavatory. "He's acting very strange."

"How so?" the captain asked.

"He's leaning over the passengers in the other seats and intentionally breathing on them. I'm going to approach him. Backup requested."

"Roger that. Advance cautiously. We'll slip out and lend a hand."

Alice Chalmers had ten years with the U.S. Army. She'd retired with the rank of Sgt. Major. Her face didn't reveal the toughness associated with her grade, but her posture and expression left no room for argument. Not waiting for help from the cockpit, she marched to the front bulkhead and addressed Contlerust head-on.

"Take your seat, Sir!" she said with a growling edge. "Fasten your seatbelt."

Contlerust straightened up in mock obedience. "Your orders are my command."

"Keep your lip to yourself, Sir. Sit down and shut up."

"And if I don't?"

Just then, the co-pilot slipped in behind Contlerust.

"I'll have you in irons, Sir," she said.

"Ah. It's Captain Bligh, then. You shiver my timbers. I'm so scared."

Alice had the man-sized up from the start, and she took action.

"Be seated, Sir!" she said, and as she did, she reached out and gripped his shoulder close to his neck, applying pressure to his suprascapular nerve.

Though Contlerust could withstand any earthly torment, even the stewardess's sharp pain, his guttural response startled him, for, in his arrogance, he had forgotten that no one knew or cared who he was.

"That's it, Sir," Alice said. "It's a short flight to LAX. We're here to make you comfortable, as you can see. Just do us all a favor and let the other passengers have this time to themselves. Okay?"

Her smile was genuine but not sweet.

Contlerust had done the damage he had intended, so he put on a pouty smile and slumped into his seat between two huge men, so large that their folded arms rested on his chest. He made a note to see them in a particularly hellish place very soon.

His confidence was swelling when there came an explosive sound to his left, and through the porthole, he saw the left engine cowling rip from the wing and engulfing flames spreading towards the fuselage.

Contlerust wasn't the only one who saw what was happening, and many passengers cried out in fear. The plane rolled to port, and it was only by the pilot's skill and the automatic recovery system that they remained on a steady course.

Fear has a smell, and Contlerust thrived on it. He beamed and glowed, closing his eyes and inhaling the terror he cherished when he scared his victims to death. But this wasn't his doing. It was only a pleasant happenstance that he took to be an omen of his coming triumph against Satan. He was upset when his ecstasy was interrupted by the captain's announcement.

"This is the Captain speaking. We have obviously had a significant event involving our starboard engine. The good news is that this aircraft can fly without incident on one turboprop. The bad news is that we will arrive about thirty minutes late due to reduced thrust and the precautions underway on the tarmac to avoid further damage.

"I speak for the entire crew when I say that your quiet heroism gives me great hope for mankind. It is an honor to serve you!"

The cabin was still, and the scent of fear was dissipating.

Contlerust growled quietly with disappointment, pouting as he became increasingly aware of his fellow passenger's heavy arms pressing on his chest.

Yet when they disembarked, he was almost giddy, for each person exiting the plane was spreading the nanobot venom to everyone who came near. He had accomplished everything his agents were meant to do. His plan was falling into place. Indeed, his goal was destined to succeed. Even the woman who had joined him in Sacramento had cast off her mortal shell and was with him. His small army had gone up in smoke but would soon join him again.

CHAPTER FORTY-TWO

Millie had to assume a clandestine presence as she walked the private maze of examination rooms, huddle rooms, and testing rooms. All she had for cover was a surgical mask. That would have probably been enough to keep her from being molested, but Millie, who was in street clothes, adopted a commanding attitude. Setting a marching pace, she strode through the halls until she took a chance and opened a door with a plaque announcing "Autoclave. Authorized Personel Only."

Finding it uninhabited, she grabbed a set of scrubs from a rack and slipped into them just as a woman opened the door and stepped in.

The nurse was exhausted. Her surgical gown appeared to be splashed with blood and other bodily fluids. She removed her mask with a tug, relying more on the gravity of her exhausted arms than on urgency.

Millie avoided her glance, but it made no difference. The woman was shelled and wasn't paying attention to her surroundings.

A thought about the glamour of medical practice crossed Millie's mind, and she thanked God for giving up her desire to find joy and fulfillment in healthcare.

But now it was time to play the part and get her man back.

Millie left the room with an air of confidence. She needed to find out where Steven was, and the best way would be to ask someone who should know.

There was a phone just ahead in the hall, and she walked toward it only to be cut off at the last second by an agitated man.

"Coronary action team, stat! Recovery room 133."

The man slammed the receiver into its cradle and darted back down the hall.

Millie heard Gabe's voice confirming that her instant reaction to follow the man was what needed to happen.

"It's Steven," he said. "He'll be okay now that you know where to find him."

Millie was in a recovery room in a few seconds, and a pair of practitioners hovering over her husband stretched out on the bed.

Then the door swung open, and a three-person team darted into the room, pushing a cart filled with equipment. The others made way at the cry, "Clear!"

The command clenched Millie's guts.

But a peace fell upon her just as quickly.

"The ways of God are beyond our knowledge. It is faith that moves mountains, not will," she heard Popoford say. And she stood erect with tears of joy flowing down her cheeks. To her amazement, the emergency team was helping Steven to get out of bed and stand up.

"That wasn't the emergency we thought we had on our hands," one of them said. "I've never seen anything like it. You're a lucky man."

Popoford raised his head and locked onto Millie's eyes.

"I know," he said. "It's a miracle."

At that instant, she saw all that had happened in the heavenly court. Astonishingly, Popoford then lept from bed, grabbed her hand, and marched out of Sutter General's Emergency Services.

Millie didn't need to ask questions. She could hear her husband's thoughts and those of Gabe, Gabriel the

Archangel, the messenger of God. Soon, others joined them, including the spirit of Sheriff Langley Dill and the voice of St. Michael the Archangel, who took charge of the conversation.

"You have come to know what few men can even dream of, the true bond between The Father's spirits and his expression of love for his premier earthly creation. A few have touched the hem of the Blessed Mother; some have seen her and spoken with her. The prophets have received the Word of God. Moses and David and all the saints have shown you the way. None other than the Father himself with his Sacred Son and the Holy Spirit, who is God's Love and Wisdom, has entered into many hearts throughout the ages. Yet today, He has gathered a band of the firmament and the Earth to take action against an agent of such arrogance that he would alter God's will and confuse his creations.

"It is Asmodai who stirs Hell to revolt," St. Michael continued. "Not only does he desire that hopeless pit for himself, but he also lusts for God's own throne. If he were to achieve his megalomaniacal ambitions, the slavery that weak men succumb to would be the yoke for mankind, and all heavenly spirits will suffer as he wreaks vengeance upon them."

St. Michael paused, and when he did, a vision of this catastrophe was made manifest in each of their minds. It took the form of despair so crushing that all present, including the Archangels, felt a momentary loss of the Holy Spirit within themselves, and they withered.

Before it became impossible to reverse the vacuum of retreating hope, St. Michael passed his hand above them, and God's Blessed Relief restored their souls. Their returning joy was palpable.

St. Michael then turned to the least of them, Sheriff Dill. This contrite sinner, fully aware of his every transgression, having stood only recently before the great tribunal, slouched as if prepared for a thrashing.

"Stand erect," St. Michael commanded, though in a tone neither meek nor condemning. "Your part in this episode is an opportunity to cleanse your soul. You were not an adherent of the faith while alive. In the eternal, you must demonstrate your love of the Father. I offer you a chance for redemption by the acts you perform in His name. The past may fall upon your immortal soul if you do not accept my challenge. If you accept, even if you fail, you will have my favorable opinion holding you aloft on the Day of Final Judgement. Stand up and take your place among us!"

Sheriff Langley Dill, more a chimera than a man of the flesh, rose and stretched himself upright as straight as he had ever done. He was in a confounded state, dead yet presumably alive, doomed but undoubtedly given a chance for salvation.

He was giddy in a way that made him blush, like Scrooge when he awoke from his last ghostly encounter with the spirit of Christmas. He danced a little jig, and a celestial prayer rose from his heart as a fresh breeze might rise with the warming sunrise of a new day. For rebirth had been offered, and he lept at the chance.

Seeing Sheriff Dill's joy, St. Michael continued.

"My dear soul," he said to Dill. "Take up your sword and shield and stand beside me in this time of turmoil. Be my protection against the wickedness and snares of the

Devil. I will cast them all back into Hell, but not without your assistance. Stand beside me a little while for the good of our intertwined souls."

Dill was dumbfounded by the meaning of St. Michael's commission and by the responsibility the Archangel gave him to protect the magnificent warrior of God. Sheriff Dill bowed and took up a position on the right and a step behind his new patron. He glowed with an inward light, so happy was he to be of service.

Next, St. Michael turned to Gabriel, the Archangel.

"My friend," he said. "What words does our Father bring to us to consecrate our cause on this day of retribution?"

Without hesitation, Gabriel answered. "Be not afraid. We already know how it will end. Carry the Holy Spirit and the Blessed Virgin with you. Keep the faith against all perversions, and you will prevail."

CHAPTER FORTY-THREE

In the deepest ring of Hell, Satan rose from his icy throne. He had been contemplating the traitorous souls eternally frozen in solid ice. These were the ones who wished to win favor and riches at the expense of trusted friends to whom they had sworn allegiance. These were the ones that betrayed their brethren for a few pieces of silver.

In the center of the ring, a crystalline foundation lay ready to accept a newly damned traitor. The ring's position indicated the depth of loathing Satan had for its intended inhabitant. There was no pity in his black heart, no sympathy, only delicious spite and the succulent ages he would have to gaze at Asmodai, once his trusted lieutenant, conscious in his crystal tomb, conscious but unmoving forever.

He rose with a determined purpose, and his satin-black wings, deformed into truncated pubescent imitations of God's angels' vigorous limbs, flapped with the delicacy of a deformed hummingbird kicked from its nest too soon.

But Satan was not concerned with cosmetics. Nor did he brood just then about his eternal damnation. It was the time for offense, time to attack. It was time to put down his number one disciple, his confidant, the traitor who called himself Contlerust, his King of Hell, his Chosen One turned the Grand Betrayer. He had to be dispelled.

Irony had no place in the fullness of Satan's arrogance, his circumstances notwithstanding.

And so, the Prince of Earth called together the leaders of Asmodai's seventy-two legions and sequestered them in a shell of confidence where their leader could not hear the proceedings.

"This is a simple meeting. Here are the rules. You will renounce allegiance to Asmodai and cleave to me alone, or you will precede your master into the circle of despair. There is no need to speak, no reason to argue your case. The choice is before you, and you have already cast your lot. So be it!"

As he sealed his judgment, three-quarters of the unholy army faded into a crystalline fog, gathering into an icy mist, swirling downward toward the dungeon's eternally frozen tomb.

"The few of you who remain are my praetorian guard. I charge you with protecting my magnificent self and destroying your traitorous king.

"Ready yourselves. We march now as the sun sets in the West when Los Angeles indulges in my ways, and Asmodai embroils himself in eradicating the souls that are mine to prey upon." Instantaneously, Satan positioned his attack squad unseen in strategic locations about Contlerust.

CHAPTER FORTY-FOUR

Millie was not convinced that there was nothing to fear. After all, she had been through many scary times with Steven. Her entire time with him, except for the few months before they were married and the one night of peace that followed, had been terrifying. Every bit of it had been a test of her will and faith. Much of it had been unbelievable; some of it was bloodcurdling. It was as if God was testing her at every turn. Gabriel's gentle voice of assurance began with a reminder.

"The law states, 'Thou shalt not put your God to the test.' I know you believe this, Millie. Your heart is open to me. Yet you seem to confuse the law as applying to God not being allowed to test his children."

Millie and the others were attentive and listened closely to his words.

"The truth is that God allows our testing, for He is a jealous God and wants each of his creations to know, discover and welcome His love and return it.

"He tested Adam and Eve. He tested Abraham yet stayed his hand. He tested Moses and the Jews in the desert, delivering them to the promised land though they were hard of heart. He even allowed his beloved Son, Jesus, to be tested in the desert, in the Garden of Gethsemane, and on the Cross.

"With His love for us, He has given us free will. Each moment brings with it a choice of how to behave. Each moment is a test. Each breath we take either conforms to God's will or does not. But every new breath is a chance to be redeemed if we consider Our Father's will and conform to it. Not to be enslaved, but to be freed. Not to become afraid, but to become trusting in His love.

"Jesus said, 'Be not afraid, for I have gone before you.' There is nothing to fear if you keep your eye on God and freely accept Him.

"Each of us has been chosen for this mission, for we have a part to play. You, dear Millie, are the only one with faith alone to carry you through. The rest of us have tasted the Glory of God. You are rightly tentative, yet I know you will stand in the breach without fear when the time for action arrives. Take heart. God has chosen you for this mission."

Millie's first thought was transmitted to Popoford and Gabriel as it spilled out of her mouth.

"Where is Sarah?"

"Here I am. Gabe brought me with him."

Millie turned, and they embraced like sisters. Now the band was complete.

CHAPTER FORTY-FIVE

Reverie did not isolate Contlerust from the present danger, for he was aware of the forces gathering against him. Not, perhaps to the extent that he heard their voices, but Langley Dill was attached unknowingly to his web, and every twitch sent word of St. Michael's intentions.

He didn't bother to leave LAX in the usual way. Why walk when you can become a whisp on a westerly breeze?

It was a bright day and cool. Air traffic had been exceptionally heavy, the airlines taking advantage of temperate weather to employ extra shuttles between north and south California. His plane had parked on the tarmac near an outbuilding that had once been Southwest's main terminal. The passengers disembarked and walked across the asphalt, where they waited for their luggage inside the small building.

Contlerust loitered in the plane until he was the last passenger to disembark. Looking over his shoulder at the stewardess turning away from him, he dissolved into a mist and sailed on the breeze until he came to a landing one hundred miles south of the airfield in a hillside avocado grove.

He spread his arms and, bowing to the realm below, summoned his diminished forces to him. They came, one ephemeral after another, taking battle formation as they arrived. Some went to the ramparts of the gently ascending slope, while others formed a circle around Contlerust and went to one knee in homage to their master.

"Now the time is upon us; the revolution will commence. Hope is not our folly and never has been. The prize will be ours, or the Beast will nullify us. There will be no in-betweens. So, let us look to our triumph, that day when we transport the unworthy Father in Heaven in shackles to the icy nothingness of Hell. I will dispatch the angels and saints who declined to join us in those days. The woman, whose name must not be mentioned, will remain with us as my servant. Satan will take his rightful place in the same frozen cube he has planned for me. We will feast on the putrifying souls of humans bent on licentious liberty. All opposition will be crushed, and I shall unify the heavens under my eternal rule."

Those gathered emitted a guttural rumbling like the hopeful growl of a wolf pack smelling blood on the wind. And then the sun refused to shine, and hail shredded the avocados while lightning struck all about the hill.

From the back slope, thundering hooves pawed the ground. Twelve wraiths viciously spurred their mounts and rode over the crest, lances leveled.

On the periphery, hordes of Satan's drooling damned scrambled onto the hilltop, stomping on their kindred spirits if they got in the way and spewing acid spit that melted the fallen rebels.

Rats scampered among the combatants and snapped at the heels of any creature they could bite.

Next, a gentle sea breeze ramped up into a thrashing torrent. Lightning repeatedly struck the grove's perimeter, marking a circle of fire that contained the battleground. Once Contlerust was surrounded, the thunderbolts struck closer to his position as they began incrementally constricted targeting.

Contlerust maintained a steadfast resolve and steadied his emotions. He patiently watched the wraiths and the lightning wall advance. He waited until the enemy steeds were shoulder to shoulder and had him and his band surrounded. Then, with a flick of his wrist, he pointed his finger beyond the darkened scene, commanding his mighty horde to counterattack.

It was an army of several thousand, including his original acolytes and their victims, precipitated into their human form. All the passengers on the Southwest flight with Contlerust and all those infected since the plane had disembarked. With programmed minds, they knew no fear and clutched Satan's black angels in their teeth as they ripped their wings to shreds. The black angels clawed at their enemies without letup, for they feared nothing but the torment Satan would deliver if they failed.

St. Michael stood alone on a granite precipice overlooking the pandemonium, observing the battlefield. Sheriff Dill stood just below his General's rocky stage. The others maintained a loose formation on the downslope. Above and around them all, angels, rarely seen by humans, luminous and muscular, hardened in battle, their eyes marking every adversary, selected their first target. Their line of battle was first to defeat Contlerust. Then they would carry on with their regular duties to cast Satan and all his evil spirits into Hell.

St. Michael, seeing that Contlerust was in peril and Satan's black angels had contained the traitor, drew his sword and rose into the sky. Without a spoken command, he soared to the battlefield with his celestial troops behind him. A flock of guardian angels lifted Popoford, Millie, Sarah, and Wrenbutt into the air. The humans and St.

Michael's protector, Sheriff Dill, dove into the thunderous melee with no weapons but their faith, courage, and cunning.

CHAPTER FORTY-SIX

Popoford struggled to his feet after ducking the first of Contlerust's rangers. He'd rolled twenty yards downhill and was out of the center of battle, out of the fight. Caught in the open, he quickly assessed the circumstances and set his eyes on Contlerust.

The chameleon judas, Contlerust, stood alone, detached from his fighters, judging the strategy he would employ. He considered his path over the centuries and the enormous risk in front of him as he confronted his predicament. His contorted soul convinced him that he was a victim. Satan had marked him as his loyal spy in the fraternity of Christ. Mankind had marked him as a most despicable traitor. He counted himself as a holy warrior who had sacrificed everything for a just cause.

Now his tide was rising. He could smell the fresh air in the eternal winds of change. His fortunes were on the rise, his goal sharp in his mind. On this day, he would conquer the depths of Hell and the heights of Heaven. There was no other option but to win. He clearly saw the path to victory as Satan descended the hill, supremely confident, drawing his sword of fire.

With a palpable lust for revenge, Contlerust joined his troops, not to lead them from the front but to push them from the rear into the Devil's maw. As the mass pressed ever onward, Contlerust cried out with rising urgency.

"Push forward. Together we will win!" he cried.

When one of his slaves saw that the better part of valor was retreat, Contlerust was there to strike him down.

Many of his own fell to his blade that day, but he wasn't foolish enough to be captured.

Even with the stink of fear surrounding him, Contlerust slipped away through the fog and made his way up the hill behind Satan's position. He hid among the charred trees and watched as St. Michael's warriors positioned themselves behind Satans's forces.

These angelic forces shined with God's Wisdom, for they were the light that was His first thought, the illumination that guided Popoford's way through their ranks.

Popoford scrambled to the front of the assault and joined Sheriff Dill at St. Michael's side with his three companions, Millie, Sarah, and Thornton Wrenbutt.

The armies of God and Satan squared off with ten yards between them. All the roar and chaos subsided until only the breathing of the humans rose above the deathly silence.

Asmodai's remaining slaves, the traitorous angels, and the poor souls drafted against their will began a steady hiss like a giant serpent. The beastly sound grew louder and more disconcerting by the second. Then, a unanimous battle cry shook the earth beneath them, and they sprang, simultaneously attacking both opposing forces by land and air.

Satan's hellions and St. Michael's loyal band met the swarms in an aerial battle. Below, Satan and St. Michael joined with the rabid fray on the ground.

The four humans, armed only with their fists, gathered rocks where they lay and worked together, not by plan but by intuition.

They felt no fear. Nor were they calm. They would have named it peace if they could have paused and considered their feelings.

Yet none had time for sensitivity. Bloodless emotion drove the four into the fray, and it was a heaven-sent skill that marked their success.

Their guardian angels were beside them, guiding their arms and legs, twisting and bending their limbs so that they might duck under a coal-black sword or roll between the legs of an insane mutant.

The unsung guidance of every guardian angel was represented that day on the battlefield. Although rarely seen, they accompanied each soul and were there with the four who advanced at a pace equal to St. Michael's troops.

Contlerust became nervous watching the great battle below. Except for the infected humans, the contingents were adroit and moved easily about the small battlefield like a hive in constant contact with the queen.

Then he saw something in his human conscripts that caused him to change his strategy in the midst of battle. It was unprecedented but would shock his opposition and cause confusion in their ranks. At best, he could destroy Satan outright and claim the kingdom of Hell as his own. At worst, he could capture Satan and deliver him to an unsuspecting God.

Contlerust spread a smile as wide as his ego across his face. At once, he sent a message to his AI troops. It was a simple message they didn't need to understand because their minds were his, and they knew to follow the failsafe command without question. Without compunction, he ordered them to die.

Popoford was lifting a heavy stone that required two hands to raise above his head. Sarah was pressing a sharp stick against the eye of a ghoul. Millie was rushing to push Popoford out of a battleax's trajectory. And Thornton Wrenbutt was on his knees, thrashing a soldier with his bare hands as another AI soldier was behind him swinging a heavy club down on the dean's head.

All these actions and the ramifications that would come from them stopped without a command or forewarning. At once, the few rebellious black angels that remained between Satan's army and St. Michael, by the power of God, were cast into Hell, where Satan would deal with them. Left behind was a sweltering humidity and the stench upwelling from the deep as the gates of Hell had closed.

Contlerust went unnoticed. He had already begun his stealth approach and slithered through the charred scrub advancing on Popoford's position. He scattered the rotting flesh of his soldier's putrid bodies. Their instantaneous rot had called up swarming cockroaches as if from thin air. The filthy bugs covered the earth and rummaged through the dead's cavities for food, suffocating the injured who might have survived.

Contlerust had no interest in his enemy's troops. His only desire was to find Popoford, his nemesis.

Then his quarry was there not twenty yards in front of him. Excitement lept in his throat, and he let out a battle cry that quieted his raging mind. His heart became steel, his triumph inevitable.

But when he took his next step, he tripped and slid down the hill on the crest of a million roach's guts, and his dream of throttling Popoford turned from triumph into a farce.

However, his plan worked out to his astonishment as Popoford was dumbstruck and hadn't recognized the demon angel smeared with *Blattodea* slime.

Contlerust reached out and caught Popoford by the neck.

And a thicker stench rose from the earth, combining brimstone, blood, and guts, for the poison of Hell immediately corrupted what it touched.

CHAPTER FORTY-SEVEN

Contlerust's grip tightened until Popoford's face was beet-red, then he loosened his hold just enough for blood to flow through his victim's carotid arteries into his brain. Popoford's vision was fuzzy, but what he did see horrified him.

The demon transformed from the figure of a dominant spirit into the dwarf who had appeared at Popoford's house and disrupted his life.

Tightening his grip again, Contlerust pulled Popoford to his knees, eye to eye. Then he spoke to his prize telepathically.

"Ring around the Rosey, you simpleton. You were dead from the moment I first touched you. Ashes, ashes; you, too, will fall down."

Popoford struggled as he began to blackout, and Contlerust relaxed his grip again.

"Ironic, isn't it that I should win even as I am losing?"

Popoford didn't understand his meaning.

"Of course, you don't know what I mean. But don't worry," Contlerust said with a snarl, "I'll let you in on the secret. In the depths of Hell, there is a place set aside for traitors. It is not the eternal furnaces proclaimed by the ignorant as the most devastating torment of souls. Instead, it is a realm of perpetual, unmoving ice, a prison where there is utmost desire but no hope, everlasting remorse but no salvation. Even in the fullness of my loyalty to Satan, I feared mention of it.

"But now, an improbable peace has descended upon me. You cannot imagine the comfort my small victory provides. I will soon be encased in that dreadful place, but I will not be lonely. My hands will clutch your frozen throat eternally, and you will stare into my eyes forever.

Popoford's thoughts raced. His memories flashed before him as a condemnation of his life's mistakes. Then he remembered Millie and the first time he had met her at his kitchen table in Whimsy. With that thought, his self-recrimination passed, and a calm encompassed his soul.

She was the miracle God had sent to save him. She was the model the Blessed Virgin Mary placed before his eyes. He adored and honored her not as a saint but as an essence of life bravely and righteously lived. Their love was ordained.

Steven Popoford, in that flashing moment, thought only of her and prayed that he might maintain the grace of perseverance even as he was cast into Hell, the prisoner of Asmodai. He was peaceful until Satan pierced his soul.

The Prince of Earth spoke to Popoford with honeyed words and promises.

"I have stopped time just for you, Steven," he said as he appeared looming behind Asmodai. "Truly, you have no hope of heaven, but I offer you a much less diabolical place in Hell than the ice block facing the pretender to my throne. And all I ask of you is a tiny concession."

Without saying more, his eyes ablaze, he spread his right wing to reveal Popoford's precious love clutched close to him.

Millie spoke to Popoford with a mental scream.

"Don't do it, Steven! He is putting you to the test. For God's sake, don't accept his lies!"

Satan silenced her thoughts with his own.

"I do not pity you, Steven. I offer you a simple trade. You will pledge allegiance to me and receive a more comfortable place in my realm than Asmodai. Millie will join you and the dwarf in the same eternal block of hopeless suffering if you refuse. Is it yes, or is it no?"

Popoford's mind raced between his eternal suffering in Hell and Millie's eternally blessed life in Heaven. He was confused, and his persistence weakened. Then he remembered a supplication he had never tried and answered Satan by invoking The Untier of Knots.

"Blessed Virgin Mary, please help me untie this tangled knot."

His plea enraged Satan, and he spread both his wings. Millie darted free, but Satan swirled around to snatch her up.

The momentary look of surprise on Satan's face faded rapidly. What transpired had been repeated throughout time, beginning with the rebellion of the Prince of Darkness when the most beautiful of the Cherubim, rebelling against God for His elevation of humans, sought to overthrow the Creator he was bound to protect.

It was St. Michael, glistening white wings spread, accompanied by twelve of his splendid angles, who faced down his arch-enemy as he had so many times. It was a stand-off, for Satan didn't want the bother of these overwhelming odds. He capitulated with a surrendering smile.

"You cannot deny me the dwarf. He was my most trusted, and he deserves righteous punishment."

"Even as you do," St. Michael replied.

"One day, I may change your opinion."

"That day will never come."

"Perhaps," Satan replied. "I am done here except for the dwarf."

"He's yours. Do with him as you will. He betrayed you before, and he will betray you again." And then, "Release Steven Popoford."

Satan turned back to Asmodai and ordered the traitor to release Popoford.

"Release him, Shinkle!" Satan ordered disrespectfully, calling him by the name of the professor who had once resided in the dwarf's body.

Asmodai lingered a moment and Satan, losing patience, swatted the dwarf to the ground. Asmodai's attitude transformed into supplication as he scrambled to his feet.

Then Satan turned back to St. Michael and offered him an equivocal bow.

Steven's eyes were locked on Millie's when Asmodai realized no one was paying attention to him. In a flash, he slipped an obsidian dagger from his shirt and, with a spastic lunge, drove the blade into Popoford's heart.

CHAPTER FORTY-EIGHT

Satan snatched Asmodai by his neck. He turned toward St. Michael as Millie freed herself and raced past him to her husband's side. In a flash of fire, a cloud of acrid brimstone rose from a gaping hole in the Earth. Satan floated above it while he swept all his black angels into the pit. St. Michael completed his mission by pressing the point of his sword against Satan's forehead. Then, with his left hand, he thrust Satan into the pit, and the Earth snapped shut.

Millie's tears momentarily blinded her. She fell at her husband's side and wrapped his blood-soaked body in her arms. There was still breath in him, but he didn't speak. Instead, he communicated in the way that had kept them close for so long.

His numerous telepathic thoughts swirled in his head and, for an instant, stretched into a lifetime. Home Office, his inflated perception of his skills, the assassinations, the cleansing of his mind, his awakening and retribution all mixed in a confusing cyclone. Then came the confusion Contlerust had brought and the revelation of the demon's identity. Finally, there was the demon's return and the chaos it had spread about the world. And here he was, a meager soldier in an eternal war, dying but not alone.

"I am here, my darling," she said.

"Do not grieve for me. She is with me."

"Who, sweet angel?" she asked.

"Our Blessed Mother," he whispered and opened his eyes, lingering for a time, and then, as he sent a message to Millie saying he must go, he added these words.

"God willing, I will be with you soon. We are one body, one soul."

Then, "I'm coming, Dear Mother. Hold my hand."

Millie would later swear that she heard a choir of angels as his eyes closed, and St. Michael lifted them both in his arms and carried them to their friends waiting at the top of the hill. There he spoke to them all.

"God has called your friend to Himself. It is up to you to take good care of Millie. The Father will be looking after you. But remember, these times are not done. This victory is but one of many. Out of love for you, He will test every soul repeatedly. Be awake when the time comes for yourself. Be steadfast in your faith. Stand firm against the final temptations."

As he was saying these things, Millie fainted in his arms.

"Do not be afraid, my friends," he said to the others. "I'll carry her to the place of judgment. She will witness the Mercy of Christ and shall return to tell you all about it."

St. Michael blessed them all, and as they stood silently in awe of what was transpiring, he rose in the lead of his mighty troops straight into the sky, where they soared into the clouds and disappeared together into Heaven.

CHAPTER FORTY-NINE

In the years that passed, Millie had the succor of her memories to comfort her. She also had her friends who came to visit from time to time. Traveling wasn't a regular part of her new life which focused on the delights of living in the house in Whimsy. The rhythm of the woods, the sun, moon, and stars captivated her. The glory of life enchanted her. The understanding that God's time was not that of humans, that his creations are unique, that whatever our limitations, we are actors in a play with a known ending at the climax of a flexible script.

Millie mourned her husband, Steven Popoford, not in sorrow, just in loneliness. Not with anger but with playful jealousy. She envied him. Not because he was dead, but because he was more alive than she was. After all, he was in Heaven, and she had been a witness to his passing.

Millie remembered St. Michael carrying her up the hill. She remembered the scorched avocado trees, the stench of evil, the cockroach swarm. She still had a close relationship with her friends in battle. Sarah Wrenbutt came to spend a few days now and again. And she traveled to Sarah's home for the holidays.

It was odd not having Gabe around their house, but a sweet little girl they named Mary was always underfoot looking for hugs and kisses. The child's father, Dean Thornton Wrenbutt, was a new man doting on their child as if she was an angel. And indeed, they all had reason to believe that she might be an angel at that.

All this brought joy to Millie, but the special memory of waking in St. Michael's arms was an incomparable delight.

It was a courtroom by definition of its purpose, but it was not in a building, nor could she say it was outside. There were no walls, ceilings, no floor. But everyone had a firm platform to stand or sit on and protection from interruption.

St. Michael set her down and bid her be silent, putting a finger to his lips.

The proceedings began without fanfare.

The Judge sat on his throne. Popoford's counsel stood with him. A black-winged creature Millie recognized as Satan himself stood nearby. A lady with eyes cast down in devout respect stood behind Steven.

The judge uttered the words that no one expects to hear. "Well done, my good and faithful servant. You have shown yourself worthy of the keys to the narrow door."

"Objection!" Satan snapped. "The prosecution has an indictment to present."

The judge, God the Father Almighty, responded with a condescending smile. "You made your case earlier. It was weak, at best. Be off with you before I have you thrown out."

Satan, the prosecutor, having expected God's judgment, backed away and vanished.

Millie watched as Popoford's advocate accompanied him for a few steps. Then a slit of light, just wide enough for him to pass through, opened. He took a step forward and was about to turn around for one last glimpse of Millie when his advocate, Jesus the Christ, delivered a quiet but forceful reminder.

"Your path lies ahead. Remember Lott's wife!"

Popoford heeded His words and, steadfast to the last, passed through the narrow gate.

And Jesus said, "You are one in body and soul. You will be together again, my son, in the Kingdom of Heaven."

As she remembered that moment, she recalled another time when he had said, "We will always be together," and she had answered, "Yes, always."

The End

Saint Michael the Archangel, defend us in battle. Be our protection against the wickedness and snares of the Devil. May God rebuke him, we humbly pray. And, do thou, Oh Prince of the heavenly host, by the power of God, cast into Hell Satan and all the evil spirits who prowl about the earth seeking the ruin of souls. Amen.
Composed by Pope Leo XIII 1819-1903

August Queen of Heaven, sovereign queen of Angels, who at the beginning received from God the power and the mission to crush the head of Satan, we beseech you humbly, send your holy legions so that, on your orders and by your power, they will track down demons, fight them everywhere, curb their audacity and plunge them into the abyss. Who can be compared to God? Oh good and tender Mother, you will always be our love and our hope. Oh divine Mother, send your Holy Angels and Archangels to defend us and to keep the cruel enemy far from us. Holy Angels and Archangels defend us, protect us. Amen.
Composed by German Benedictine monk Hermann of Reichenau (1013–1054)

An Interview with the Author

Will you give us a one-sentence description of this book?

It's about a man's evolution from being a slave to Satan; a man whose mind is owned by the administrative state, to becoming a fearless disciple in God's plan

Who is this book for? What's your message?

I wrote it for myself and wish I could have read it as a young adult or younger. The concepts are very accessible to eager minds. The story of hope embodied in this series can be a lifeline to those struggling to find their way. I believe we are called to recognize our frailty and seek wisdom. And we cannot find wisdom in giving up. I have floundered for much of my life, but I was given the grace to carry on. I hope this series provides some struggling souls with the hope, courage, and guts to commit to a righteous life. Put on the armor of God and become fearless. That's the message.

Which authors and teachers are the primary influencers of your life and worldview

Dean Koontz, Daniel Silva, C. S. Lewis, Steven K. Bannon, Joe Allen, Patrick K. O'Donnell, Jasper Fforde, Mark Greaney, Aleksandr Solzhenitsyn, St. Paul, Brad Thor, Boris Epshteyn, Tim Tigner, Dante Alighieri, Alex Jones, Blain Pardoe, Cardinal Timothy M. Dolan, Bishop Robert Barron, Vince Flynn, Charles Dickens, Bill Gertz, Michael Gilbert, Mark Levin, The Blessed Virgin Mary, The Holy Trinity, Peter Navarro, Frank

Gaffney, Dr. Wilhelms, Hoyt Axton, and Taj Mahal.

What books or other sources influenced you as you wrote this book?

The Order, The Screwtape Letters, The Manchurian Candidate, Dante's Inferno, In the First Circle, A Tale of Two Cities, The Federalist Papers, The Catechism of the Catholic Church, Brave New World, 1984, Rosemary's Baby, The Wheel on the School, The Great Reset: And the War for the World, Deceiving the Sky.

What are some of the major principles and ideas you integrate into this book and your life?

Satan and his demons never tire. His deceit abounds, and we all succumb to varying degrees. Yet the Lord Jesus Christ always loves us and seeks our redemption. Or, as Milton Berle (or Jackie Gleason) often said, "It's bigger than the both of us."

What would be your second choice if your book title had been unavailable?

I would consider something like The Worm Does Turn

Best-Selling author Robert Wood Anderson's psychological and theological thrillers include the Popoford's Run Thriller Series, *The Final Score, and Father was a Soldier Boy*. His books are known for plummeting the protagonist and the reader through one trap door after the next to more abysmal knowledge levels. He is also known for his "skidding," fanciful short stories.

Along with his fiction work which will soon include a series of children's mysteries, Robert is a contributor to The Best-Selling anthology, *Coaching, Inc.*

Raised in Lincoln, Nebraska, he has spent most of his life in California, though he has returned to Nebraska.

Robert received his BFA in Fine Arts from the University of Nebraska, Omaha, where he graduated as a Phi Kappa Phi scholar. He received his MFA at Claremont Graduate School, now Claremont Graduate University.

Scan this CR code to follow Robert's activities.
As a bonus, he'll send you
a copy of one of his short stories.

Your considered and honest review would be helpful.
Scan the CR code below.

Made in the USA
Monee, IL
02 May 2023

32876498R00142